HELL IS FOR REAL

A Little Boy's Incredible Journey To Hell... and BACK!

by Gary Apple

New York
www.WalnutPress.com

Published in New York, New York, by Walnut Press.

This is a work of fiction. Names, characters, businesses, organizations, places, events and incidents either are the product of the author's imagination or are used fictitiously. Any resemblance to actual persons, living or dead, events, or locales is entirely coincidental.

Cover Art and Book Design by
Angelica Yunuhen Sanchez.
www.angelicayunuhen.com

**Y**our boy drew this in art class, Mr. Bolton," said Detective Zanderhoff. "We're hoping you can explain it."

I took the sheet of paper. "This? It's just a bunch of stars."

Zanderhoff shook his head. "Don't insult us, Mr. Bolton."

"What are you talking about? They're stars. Five stars."

"They're Pentagrams, Mr. Bolton. Not stars. Pentagrams."

This entire conversation made no sense to me. "Pentagrams. Stars. What's the difference?"

"If you're trying to summon Satan there's a big difference," said Detective Zanderhoff, matter-of-factly.

"You're saying my 6-year-old boy was summoning the Devil into his art class?"

"I'm saying he drew five pentacles in the classic Sigil of Baphomet configuration. It's unmistakable. The only thing missing is the goat's head."

C⊕NTENTS

PROLOGUE
BURGER KING OF DARKNESS

L abor Day weekend means different things to different people. For some, it means that the oppressive heat of summer will be ending and the glorious season of autumn will soon be here. For kids, it means the freedom of July and August will soon be snatched away and replaced with imprisonment in a school. But for my family and me, the Labor Day weekend of 2010 was unique from all others – it's the weekend my son Davin went to Hell.

No, I don't mean he had a bad couple of days. Davin actually visited Hell. You know – Hades. The Underworld. Yeah, *that* Hell.

Before you start feeling all sorry for the boy, I should tell you that he's fine. Like Orpheus, he came out of Hell alive and in one piece. And just like Orpheus, he was missing something very important to him. I'll tell you all about that later.

You're probably wondering why a 6-year-old boy went to Hell. Or how he managed to come back. Or if this story is true. You may even be wondering why you wasted money on this book. All I can ask is that you be patient – every one of your questions will be answered (except, perhaps, the last one). I assure you, though, that everything you're about to read is absolutely true.

We live in a suburban community called Old Bethpage, on New York's Long Island. I'm by no means rich – though if this book manages to go viral, that could change. Old Bethpage is a sleepy little town with one little shopping center, an elementary school, and an obnoxious 7-11 that recently opened. As far as we know, there are no Slurpees in Hell. Although they do have those rotating hot-dog grillers (except they're really big and they have people on them).

The first hint that something out of the ordinary had happened to Davin occurred at a nearby Home Depot. I had taken the kids on an outing to buy a new gasket for the downstairs toilet. The darn thing would simply not stop running, wasting water and driving us crazy with the drip-drip-drip sound.

I said "Kids, I have to go to Home Depot to buy something for the john. Anyone want to come?" Davin came bounding down the steps – he loves Home Depot because if you break things, the workers still have to be nice to you. His 14-year-old sister, Lally, reluctantly agreed to tag along. She's at that peculiar age where hardware stores don't excite her – even big chain hardware stores. Hopefully she'll outgrow it.

Even at 6, Davin still loves to ride in shopping carts. Lally was pushing him as we passed through the floor coverings aisle and entered the garden supplies department. Suddenly, Davin shouted, "Stop!" He leaped out of the cart and ran up to a display of pitchforks and just stared at them.

"Whatcha doin' kiddo?" I asked.

And then he said something that made the hair on my arms rise.

He picked up a pitchfork and said matter-of-factly, "This is like the one Lucifer has."

"You mean Lucy, that girl in your kindergarten class?"

"No, not Lucy. Lucifer. The Lucifer I saw in Hell."

He made a few playful jabs with the pitchfork and said something that sounded like "a-rul shach kigon," then put it back on the rack and ran away to break something.

On the way home, I knew I had to ask Davin some questions. "Who wants to go to Burger King?" I asked.

"Meeeeee!" squealed Davin.

"Not me," moaned Lally. She's at that peculiar age where she doesn't like Burger King.

Davin likes the local Burger King because they have an indoor playground with colorful plastic tubes he can crawl around in. I remember when he was four, he climbed up to the top and then was afraid to move. We had to send Lally to coax the little fella down. Once safely on the ground, Davin realized he had left Mr. Peety up there. Mr. Peety is a little stuffed giraffe that Davin always has with him. And I mean ALWAYS. If we go to the Fairway Supermarket, Mr. Peety comes with us. If we go to the dentist, Mr. Peety comes with us. So Lally had to climb back up and rescue poor Mr. Peety.

As we sat at our round table eating chicken nuggets shaped like royal crowns, I decided to follow up on Davin's shocking remark. "Hey, Dav, remember when you said you saw the Devil's pitchfork?"

"Of course he remembers," said Lally, sipping her Dr. Pepper. "It was only like ten minutes ago."

"Lally, please," I cautioned. "Davin, where did you see Satan's pitchfork?"

"He doesn't like that name, Daddy," said Davin.

"What name?"

"Satan. He wants everyone to call him Lucifer. Or...." His little brow furrowed in deep thought. "Or Beetlejuice."

"Do you mean Beelzebub, Davin?" I corrected.

"Yeah, that's it. Bagelbub!" he proclaimed proudly.

Lally laughed so hard Dr. Pepper came out her nose. But I couldn't believe what I was hearing. Little Davin, a child who still slept with a light on and referred to the toilet as the potty, was talking about a personal encounter with the King of Darkness himself.

"I see," I said, trying to remain calm. "And where did you meet Sata...er, Lucifer?"

"When I was in Hell, silly," he said, and then grabbed Mr. Peety and ran off to the play area as if nothing was out of the ordinary.

Beelzebub? Hell? Pitchforks? These words wheeled round and round my mind like a carousel on a merry-go-round. Why was my little son talking about these things?

"Hey, Dad," interrupted Lally, "if Davin goes to the loony bin, can I have his room?"

CHAPTER ONE
THE FIRST PERSON YOU SEE IN HELL

ver the next few months, I'd learned more about Hell than I'd ever wanted to know. The main thing I learned was.... Well, to put it in Davin's own words, "Daddy, Hell is for real!"

I was like most people – I thought that Hell was something allegorical. You know, more of a concept than an actual place – like Atlantis or Gilligan's Island. Hell was like the Boogeyman – something made up to scare people into being good. In my wildest imagination, I never dreamed it was an actual place full of.... Well, we'll get to all that in due time. If I tell you everything at once, you'll just overload and dismiss this entire book as nonsense (if you haven't done that already). And I might as well tell you right now that, not only is there a Hell, but there is a Boogeyman. His name is Carl.... And he's the first person you see in Hell.

I learned about Carl one afternoon when I was taking Davin to ballet class. Yes, ballet. Don't get me started, okay? The kid really likes the movement and the music. Lots of normal boys like ballet. But none of them have danced it around the Fiery Pits of Damnation before.

I was driving my Honda Civic while Lally read the local paper in the passenger seat and Davin played his Nintendo

DS in the backseat. It was a few weeks after the Burger King discussion, and there'd been no further mention of Satan or Hell. I'd written the entire episode off to the runaway imagination of a 6-year-old kid.

Lally looked up from the Plainview/Old Bethpage Herald and said, "Hey! George DeCosta's in the hospital. They think a garbage truck backed over him." I knew the DeCosta kid – he was a year older than Davin and a nasty bully. Somehow DeCosta had found out about Davin's ballet class and had been tormenting my boy for weeks. Davin looked up from his game and said, "It wasn't a garbage truck. It was Carl."

I looked at Davin in my rearview mirror, trying to see if Davin was kidding. There was no hint of a smile on his face. "Who's Carl?" asked Lally before I could.

"Carl is the Boogeyman. He's the first person you see in Hell."

"What on earth are you talking about, Davin?" I asked.

"Can I have his room?" asked Lally.

"When I got to Hell, the first person I saw was the Boogeyman. He looks real scary, but he's really not that bad. Just don't get him angry. And he sweats a lot."

Over the coming months I learned there's a lot of sweating going on down in Hell.

We pulled into the parking lot of the Ackerman Dance Academy. Though it was almost class time, I had to ask Davin a few follow-up questions.

"So, you met the Boogeyman?"

"Uh, huh."

"In Hell?"

"Yeah. Did you remember to bring my rosin?"

"Yes, it's in your bag. Where was the Boogeyman?"

"Carl was right at the gate. He was trying to play a banjo," he said.

"A banjo?"

"Yeah, but his fingers are so thick he just can't do it, Dad. Can you imagine playing the banjo with really thick fingers?" He held up his little hands and spread his fingers, demonstrating what thick fingers were like.

"I can't believe this," exploded Lally. "First the fruity ballet lessons and now this! Beth Goldstein's little brother is so cool. Jeez, Dad, it's not fair."

I shot Lally a look that said, "Yes, I know this all sounds a little odd." And she shot me a look that said, "Odd? My little brother is going crackers!" And I shot her a look that said, "Stop it, okay? Just stop it. We'll deal with it."

Davin sat in the back seat watching us shoot looks back and forth. "Can I go to class now?"

"Yes, Chief. Have a good lesson."

"I'm gonna. We're learning pirouettes," he said and hopped out of the car.

But then a thought occurred to me. "Hey, Chief. How do you know it was the Boogeyman that hurt George DeCosta?"

Davin rolled his eyes as if it were the stupidest question ever asked. "He TOLD me, Dad," he said, then pranced into the Ackerman School of Dance.

Lally and I watched him go, thinking about what transpired. She shot me a glance that said, "Can I have his room?"

CHAPTER TWO
IT ALL BEGINS AT CHUCK E. CHEESE'S

At this point, you're probably wondering, "What the hell is going on?" Well, I was too, quite frankly. I confess, there has been some moderate mental illness in our family – but luckily all on my ex-wife Arlene's side. Her sister suffered from bouts of depression and took a daily dosage of Zoloft, Xanax, and some form of stinkfish extract. Also, Arlene had an Uncle Willy who received a frontal lobotomy way before it was fashionable. He was quite normal after that, though every so often, for no apparent reason he would shout, "Henderson, don't open the trunk!" We never found out what he was talking about, though after his funeral, we noticed that someone named Henderson had signed the guest registry.

I suppose I should mention that Arlene and I had divorced a couple of years after Davin was born, after I had caught her having an affair with an actuary at her job. I think she wanted to be caught, because she kept leaving little clues, like coming home without her shoes or calling me Walter on the rare occasions we were intimate (my name is Richard). She actually married this Walter fellow shortly after the divorce, which bothered me greatly. Not because I was jealous, but because Walter is the blandest, most boring individual on the face of the planet. Walter fits the classic definition of a nebbish – when he leaves a room, everyone looks up to see who came in.

But divorces happen, we agreed to joint custody, and everything was relatively normal up until Davin's 6th-birthday. We had already thrown birthday parties at home, at amusement parks, and at bowling alleys. We had put off the inevitable as long as possible. Like countless other parents, we had no choice…. it was time for a birthday party at Chuck E. Cheese's.

Let me say right now – in no uncertain terms – Chuck E. Cheese's had nothing – I repeat NOTHING – to do with the events that you will learn about in this book. It is a place of joy and laughter and safety and tasty food. Even after our son's ordeal in Hell, we went back to Chuck E. Cheese's for the food and the fun. So please – Kids, if you're a fan of Chuck E. Cheese, you keep going there, okay? Mom and Dad – Take your children there often. You won't regret it. Chuck E. Cheese's Attorneys – please don't sue me. I do not have a bad thing to say about Chuck E. Cheese. It's not my fault that this is where our story truly begins.

Davin's 6th birthday party at Chuck E. Cheese's was uneventful. Well, it actually was very eventful, but only in the normal children's-party-sort-of-way. There was spilled apple juice, dropped pizza, and one kid threw-up on the horsy ride. The courteous and professional Chuck E. Cheese's staff took it all in stride, wiping off the apple juice, picking up the pizza, and hosing down Pukey The Horse (as Lally started calling him).

Davin and his friends had the time of their lives. Arlene and I even enjoyed it, though Walter spent the whole time reading actuarial charts at a booth near the Whack-A-Mole. And when Chuck E. himself came out tossing prize tickets, the kids went into a feeding frenzy. It was such a delightful sight, that even Lally smiled (but don't tell her I told you).

But as we left the establishment, the afternoon took a strange and frightening turn.

CHAPTER THREE
PAGE CANNOT BE FOUND

We left Chuck E. Cheese's laden with birthday gifts, balloons, and prizes. Walter apparently had his share of excitement for one day, so he and Arlene went home. I piled Davin, Lally, and Mr. Peety into the back seat of my Honda Civic along with a bunch of gifts that couldn't fit in the overstuffed trunk.

Davin received a lot of cool presents – a radio controlled helicopter, a monster truck, and a pair of tap shoes from a boy in his ballet class. (Stop it. It was on his Capezio.com wish list.) But one friend who shall remain nameless gave him a box labeled "Hula Harry's Chocolate Macadamia Coconut Clusters." This box of candy practically screamed RE-GIFTED. And had Davin not opened it during the ride home, I probably would have gifted it to someone else sooner or later.

Unfortunately, Davin wasn't content with all the pizza and soda and ice cream and cotton candy he'd consumed at Chuck E. Cheese's. While I was driving home, he opened the Hula Harry's Chocolate Macadamia Coconut Clusters and ate a few.

As far as I know, Davin has never had an allergy to nuts. He practically inhales Skippy and if I bring home a bag of pistachios, I have to hide them so he won't polish them off. But there was something about the combination of macadamia nuts, coconuts, and cheap chocolate that triggered something mighty ugly in my boy. (Later, when I inspected the box, I discovered that the expiration date had been suspiciously scratched off. There was simply no way of telling how long these chocolate-covered time bombs had been snaking their way across the country.)

As we turned the corner onto our street, Davin grabbed his belly and cried, "Daddy, I don't feel well."

"Don't you dare puke on me, Davin!" shouted Lally, the picture of compassion.

Perhaps Davin didn't hear the "Don't" part of Lally's command, because he proceeded to spew all over his older sister. While the well-trained crew at Chuck E. Cheese's handles situations like this with aplomb, Lally flailed in disgust and howled like a banshee. As a father of two, I've seen some pretty vile things come out of my children. But this particular instance wins the prize. It was as if the entire two-hour birthday party was splattered over Lally – a revolting medley of pizza, chicken nuggets, cake, and Hula Harry's Chocolate Macadamia Coconut Clusters. There was even a remnant of a birthday candle lodged in Lally's hair.

Once we got home, Lally dashed into the shower and remained there until the hot water gave out. Meanwhile, Davin got worse and worse. I'll spare you the details, since nobody wants to read about a sick child. Let's just say I began to get concerned about what exactly my little boy had ingested.

I went online and Googled "Hula Harry's Chocolate Macadamia Coconut Clusters." Only two results came up. The first was a website titled: HulaHarrysChocolateMacadamiaCoconutClusters.com.

This struck me as possibly relevant, so I clicked on it.

I wasn't very surprised when this familiar message filled my screen:

Page cannot be found.
The page you are looking for might have been removed, had its name changed, or is temporarily unavailable.
HTTP 404 – File not found

The only other search result was for Abernathy & Levin Attorney's At Law. A quick visit to their site revealed that Counselors Abernathy and Levin specialized in class-action litigation. Needless to say, this set off alarms. I decided to take Davin to the hospital immediately.

CHAPTER FOUR
PRE-APPROVED

I now know that there are real Hells and virtual Hells. Though you'll learn about the real Hell soon enough, you may already be familiar with the Hospital Emergency Room Admittance Process Hell.

I carried a limp Davin into the Emergency Room of Mid-Long Island General Hospital. The poor guy was clutching Mr. Peety and moaning softly. At the Admittance Window, a spectacled woman spoke to me through a hole in piece of glass. "Can I help you?" she asked, reluctantly looking up from her Sudoko puzzle. From her blasé attitude, you would have thought I was holding a ham sandwich and not a barely conscious 6-year-old boy.

"Yes. Something's wrong with my son. I don't know what it is. I think he...."

"Is that your son?" she asked, gesturing toward Davin with her pencil.

A million sarcastic replies shot through my brain. "No, I'm a ventriloquist and he's my dummy." "No, my wife had an affair with the cable guy." "No, I found him outside. I think he fell out your window." But instinctively I knew sarcasm would only delay the process, so I simply nodded and said "Yes, his name is Davin."

She grabbed a well-used clipboard and clamped about a hundred papers under its clip. It was so thick, she was barely able to slip it through the slot at the bottom of the window. "Please fill everything out and return it to me."

"Can't someone see him now?" I asked, trying to sound reasonable.

She smiled and gestured toward the waiting room. "Sir, there are other people who need help, too." I looked around – The waiting room was empty except for some wino sleeping it off. I really didn't want to start up with her, so I took the clipboard and carried Davin over to a seat.

The forms went on FOREVER. The first four seemed reasonable enough – types of vaccinations received, medical history, allergies, family history, and so on. And then came the insurance questions – Primary Insurer, Secondary Insurer, Social Security Numbers, place of business, previous place of business, previous health insurance, previous secondary health insurance, spouse's previous secondary health insurance, and so on.

Now, I don't have the best health insurance in the world. I'm a self-employed writer, and get my health insurance through the Independent Artists and Writers Union. It's a terrific plan, unless you actually need medical attention. But one thing it does cover is emergency hospital visits, so I wasn't worried. Stupid me.

When I returned the overstuffed clipboard, the Admittance Lady looked like I was handing her a plate of week-old sushi. "Insurance card, please." I slipped my card through the slot and was instructed to have a seat.

"But what about my boy? He really needs to be looked at."

"And he will be. As soon as..." She looked down at my insurance card and stopped short. "This is the only insurance you have?"

"Yes. Why?"

"Does your wife have a different plan?"

I shook my head. "We're divorced."

She gave me a look that said "I'm not surprised."

"Any secondary insurance? Anything?" she asked, with apparently very little hope.

"No. Just this. Is what I have okay?"

She gave a little laugh that sort of creeped me out, then disappeared behind a door.

Davin and I sat for another 40 minutes, and then the place exploded with activity. The doors from the street swung open and a team of EMTs wheeled in a huge man on a gurney. The man's muscular arms were covered with homemade tattoos and his wrists were handcuffed to the rails of his gurney. Two armed officers followed in tow, one of whom went up to the Admittance Window.

"We're from N.C.C. Pizutto here got into a knife fight with another inmate."

To my amazement, Miss "There Are Other People Waiting" pressed a button, and two doors swung open wide to embrace Mr. Pizutto. He was wheeled right in!

"Now wait a minute," I sprung to my feet. "My son has

been here an hour!"

The Admittance Woman looked at me like I was a total idiot. "The County pays for everything, Mr. Bolton. His paperwork is pre-approved."

I could hear people being paged over the P.A. system to attend to Mr. Pizutto. Doctors and nurses dashed past us so swiftly, their stethoscopes flew behind in the breeze.

By this point, little Davin was either asleep or unconscious. Finally, the doors that admitted Pizutto swung open and a skinny male nurse came out to retrieve my son.

As he wheeled him back, I filled him in on the day's events, emphasizing the Hula Harry's candy. He nodded, then said, "That mouse kind of gives me the creeps."

"What mouse?" I asked, completely puzzled.

"The Chuck E. Cheese mouse. It's just some minimum-wage kid in a costume, right?"

Like I said, there are all types of Hells.

CHAPTER FIVE
SWITCHED AT DEATH

The Emergency Room was divided into sections, separated by curtains that offered just a modicum of privacy. Davin's section was tranquil compared to the activity in the neighboring station. There, Mr. Pizutto was receiving the finest and most thorough care that modern medicine had to offer. I could hear the attending physicians ordering lab work, cat scans, bone scans, x-rays, drips, drops, and transfusions. A medivac helicopter was standing by just in case they needed to fetch transplant organs

Meanwhile, Davin was attended to by a pimply-faced resident who seemed to be at the end of a 48-hour shift.

"Have you noticed any unusual behavior?" he asked me.

"Yes. He threw up his entire birthday party."

"Did he eat anything?"

This time, I couldn't refrain from sarcasm. "No. In our family, we celebrate birthdays by fasting."

"You're Jewish?"

No more sarcasm, I swore to myself. Once again, I ran down everything that transpired during this endless day. The resident ordered some blood tests, then the P.A. system blared "Code Green, Code Green" and he dashed off to join the army of experts treating the precious Mr. Pizutto. Before long, there were so many physicians that the prison guards were squeezed out, giving me the opportunity to speak with them.

"Who is that guy?" I asked.

"Raymond Pizutto. He murdered four people out in Smithtown," answered the guard.

"That we know about," added the other Guard.

"Yeah, that we know about. Son of a bitch chopped them into pieces and fed them to his Dobermans."

"Wow," I said. What else could I say. "Wow."

"Then he killed the Dobermans and chopped THEM up. Guy's a lunatic, but he's thorough. And now he's killed another prisoner. Hope the docs can keep 'em alive – this overtime's sweet."

All the while, Davin had nothing to help him but a damp Bounty towel on his forehead provided by a porter that took pity on him. By this time Arlene had arrived with Walter in tow. She held Davin's hand and spoke comforting words, while Walter sat quietly reading something called the Property/Casualty Loss Reserve Manual - Revised Edition.

The commotion next door was punctuated by someone shouting "Clear!" This was followed by a loud, electric crack and a loud thump. The lights dimmed momentarily.

"Mr. Peety," murmured Davin, "I think they want us to dance."

"Clear!" came the cry again, followed by the same blast of current. I could feel the hairs on my arm standing up from the charge.

Davin murmured something softly.

Arlene put her ear closer to Davin's mouth. "What did you say, dear?"

Davin was barely able to whisper something. Arlene stood up straight, looking pale as a ghost.

"What did he say?" I asked her.

She looked me right in the eye and said, "He said 'Henderson, don't open the trunk.'"

CHAPTER SIX
THE POWER OF PRAYER – AND THE
INTERNET   – AND MONEY

They never actually said Davin was in a coma. To tell you the truth, they avoided saying anything concrete at all. When I would ask a doctor what's wrong with my boy, they would equivocate with phrases like "Well, it might be a number of things." Or "We've ruled out Dutch Elm Disease."

The phrase "It's hard to tell" became sort of a mantra when it came to Davin.

"What's wrong with him?"

"It's hard to tell."

"Why won't he respond?"

"It's hard to tell."

"When will he wake up?"

"It's hard to tell."

I can't imagine "it's hard to tell" was an acceptable answer in med school, yet somehow it was perfectly okay around Mid-Long Island General Hospital.

Oh, there were some things they were perfectly precise about, such as how much deductible I had to pay, how many days in the hospital would be covered, what drugs had to be paid for out-of-pocket, and stuff like that. I couldn't wait for the day they asked "Mr. Bolton, when will you be paying your bill?"

"It's hard to tell," I would respond.

Of course, Raymond Pizutto was well on the road to recovery. While Davin had to share a room with some asthmatic kid who played Angry Birds all day, Pizutto was across the hall in a private room with round-the-clock guards who couldn't have been happier. All the prison staff had chipped in and bought him a huge fruit basket – the type with chocolates and cookies as well as fruit. Freshly-cut flowers would arrive daily.

But poor Davin just laid there, dead to the world. He didn't look in pain or discomfort, just, well, elsewhere.

After 3 or 4 days, poor Mr. Pizutto was reluctantly pronounced cured. The hospital staff threw a big going away party, and the guards even took off his ankle cuffs so he could dance with the Candy Stripers. If you could forget the fact that he butchered people and dogs, it was sort of a sweet send-off.

To say it was difficult for Arlene and me would be a terrible understatement. Being a powerless parent is perhaps the worst feeling in the world. So when the mass murderer was declared healthy, it triggered something fierce in me. And I decided to take matters into my own hands.

I've never been a very religious man. I don't attend church regularly – in fact, I'm not even a member of any congregation. Still, I've never dismissed the power of prayer. Call it wishful thinking, but I wanted to believe that someone, somewhere up there was paying attention and cares. So I decided to start a prayer chain.

While Arlene stayed with Davin, I went home and logged onto my Gmail account. It took me awhile to phrase things just right. Then I crossed my fingers and sent the following email to everyone I knew:

Dearest Friends,

My family and I have found ourselves in a situation that needs your help. No, I'm not asking for money or even much of your time, but I am asking for your prayers.

You see, my son Davin is in the hospital with some sort of ailment that the doctors can't seem to figure out. Perhaps, if all of you can find it in your hearts to put in a word for Davin, then maybe the powers that be will find a way to help his plight.

Any help you can send our way would be greatly appreciated.

Sincerely,
Richard Bolton

P.S.: Please forward this email to everyone you know. We need all the help we can get.

In truth, I really didn't expect much out of this email. But whoever said "The Lord works in mysterious ways" knew what he was talking about.

Three days later, the first envelope arrived with twenty

dollars in it. This puzzled me, and when more envelopes containing money arrived, I was completely baffled. What made it even stranger was that this money was coming from people I had never even heard of.

It took about two more days, and many more envelopes, before I began to see what was happening.

Somehow, the email had become viral. And, just like the game of telephone, the original message had morphed into something much different from how it began. I myself received 23 of my own emails, but by now they read:

Most Dearest Friend,

My name is Davin Bolton, a merchant in Nigeria, and I have been diagnosed with untreatable Akinkuni, a rare condition spread by the pollen of the Ixora flower. It has defiled all forms of medicine, and of this writing, dear friend, I have only but a few months to live.

As I prepare for the hereafter, I require assistance in distributing my money to those in need, as is my people's custom. I very much want to share these funds with you, dear friend. But since they are currently tied up in Nigerian Naira, your assistance is needed on a temporarily basis.

If I may press upon you to mail $20 for duties processing, I can most expeditiously unbound the funds and herewith therefore.

Remain blessed.
Davin Bolton

I was amazed. My innocent email had somehow morphed into a shameless example of Internet SPAM. But what is MORE amazing, hundreds of people actually sent me money. Over $14,000 arrived before Google cancelled my Gmail account.

I dumped it all into a wheelbarrow and paraded back to the hospital with it. As I rolled into the Emergency Room, the woman behind the Admittance Window smiled like a kid on Christmas. She pressed a button and the P.A. system once again blared, "Code Green. Code Green."

Davin would get the attention he needed.

CHAPTER SEVEN

SOMEONE IS MISSING

I can't say for sure whether it was the power of prayer, the power of money, or some combination of the two – but little Davin snapped out of it. Whatever wickedness was in those Hula Harry's Chocolate Macadamian Coconut Clusters had apparently worked its way out of his system and, within a few days, he seemed as good as new.

The doctors and nurses beamed with pride. As far as they were concerned, Davin's turnaround was a direct result of their training, intelligence, and unwavering dedication. As far as I could tell, they didn't do anything except bill me $1,000 for every "It's hard to tell." Still, Arlene and I were thrilled to have Davin back no matter how it happened, so we even managed to mutter a few "thank yous" just to get them out of the room.

Davin, for his part, seemed unfazed by his ordeal. His appetite sprang back with a vengeance and he couldn't wait to get back to his friends and his dance lessons. Yes, Davin's hospital room was filled with joy and relief, but there was one little problem...

"Where's Mr. Peety?" asked Davin.

The stuffed giraffe was with us when I brought Davin into the hospital. And all the while Davin lay in his hospital bed, Mr. Peety was snuggled up beside him. But now the little giraffe was missing, and Davin wasn't happy one bit.

"Where's Mr. Peety?!" he repeated.

"The nurses probably have him, dear," said Arlene while I dashed out to the nurse's station to find him. But as far as any of the nurses knew, Mr. Peety was still with Davin. Everyone had agreed the toy was good for the boy, so there were strict rules not to remove it.

We searched the hospital room up and down – Arlene even forced Walter to put down his trade journal and help look. But Mr. Peety simply was nowhere to be found.

I still had a wad of cash from my prayer chain SPAM thing, so I offered a $500 reward for the toy giraffe. The smell of additional cash set the entire hospital into a frenzy. I knew then how Chuck E. Cheese feels when he tosses prize tickets into the air and all the kids pounce like piranhas. (Well, piranhas don't pounce, but you know what I mean.) The entire population of the hospital ransacked the place as they scoured every nook and cranny for Mr. Peety.

Apparently the instruction to look for "a small, stuffed giraffe" wasn't quite specific enough, because people began showing up at Davin's room with all sorts of objects. People brought stuffed zebras, teddy bears, monkeys, hedgehogs, and birds of every description. One enterprising orderly brought a colostomy bag and was shocked when we broke the news that this wasn't the beloved toy. The hospital gift shop quickly sold the few stuffed giraffes it stocked. People figured that investing $8.99 for a $500 reward was good business. One little girl in a leg cast brought a picture of a giraffe she had drawn with crayons on a placemat. I was so touched, I offered her $10 but she wouldn't accept it. She gave Davin a hug and left the picture with us.

With each failed attempt to return Mr. Peety, Davin got more distraught. I promised him that we would find Mr. Peety, but in my heart I suspected he was gone for good.

As it would turn out, I would see Mr. Peety again... under conditions that were beyond unimaginable.

CHAPTER EIGHT

THE ONLY THING MISSING IS THE GOAT'S HEAD

I was working on a manuscript at the kitchen table when the phone rang.

"Mr. Bolton, this is Principal Hardly. We need you to come into school immediately."

"Is Davin okay?" I asked, worried that perhaps he'd had a relapse of some sort.

"He's not ill or injured or anything like that, but we need you to come here right now. It's very serious."

"Can you give me an idea…" *Click*. Principal Hardly had hung up.

I had no idea what was wrong. Davin had been home for a few weeks now, and other than the references to Satan's pitchfork and Carl the Boogeyman, he'd been perfectly normal. Well, he was kind of sullen over the loss of Mr. Peety, but I was sure he'd get over it sooner or later. At least I hoped so.

Since my Ex-wife has a "real job" while I'm "just a writer" who "works" from home, I'm always the one the school calls. I hopped into the Civic and rushed to Old Bethpage Elementary School which, thankfully, was not very far away. I found Davin sitting on a wooden bench in the office between two secretaries. He looked like he'd been crying.

"Hey, Chief. What's going on?"

Davin just shrugged.

Before I could press him further, a door opened and Principal Hardly stepped out. He always struck me as a friendly sort of fellow, but not today. His face was red and his bald head looked like it was under enormous pressure and in danger of exploding. I was puzzled. But then my puzzlement turned to shock when a uniformed policeman and another man in a suit appeared behind him.

"Mr. Bolton?" said the man in the suit.

"Yes?"

"We need to speak with you."

I turned toward the red Principal Hardly. "What's this about?"

"In my office, please," muttered Principal Hardly and the three men parted, allowing me to enter. I didn't know what was happening, but there was no doubt it was serious.

Once inside, I was given a chair. Principal Hardly took a seat behind his desk and the man in the suit remained standing. The police officer, whose nametag read "Gallagher," guarded the door. I guess they thought I might make a run for it.

The awkward silence was broken by the man in the suit. "Mr. Bolton, I'm Detective Zanderhoff, 3rd Precinct. Principal Bolton called us in because of the serious nature of the problem."

"What problem?" I asked, trying to sound calm.

"Detective Zanderhoff is an investigator with the Hate Crimes Division," added Principal Hardly.

"Hate Crimes? Who's guilty of a hate crime?" I asked.

"Mr. Bolton, during Miss Catugno's art class this morning, your son drew something that concerns us very much," said Zanderhoff. I had already determined that I didn't like this detective one bit. He had the self-righteous arrogance often found in people in law enforcement, politicians, and party planners. He snapped his finger and the Gallagher brought over a pink sheet of craft paper and laid it on the Principal's desk. "We're hoping you can explain this, Mr. Bolton."

I looked at the paper. It contained a drawing of five stars.

"This? It's just a bunch of stars."

Gallagher snickered and Zanderhoff just shook his head. Hardly's red head turned a deep crimson. "Don't insult us, Mr. Bolton."

"What are you talking about? They're stars. Five stars."

"They're Pentagrams, Mr. Bolton. Not stars. Pentagrams."

This entire conversation made no sense to me. "Pentagrams. Stars. What's the difference?"

"If you're trying to summon Satan there's a big difference," said Detective Zanderhoff, matter-of-factly.

"You're saying my 6-year-old boy was summoning the Devil into his art class?"

"I'm saying he drew five pentacles in the classic Sigil of Baphomet configuration. It's unmistakable. The only thing missing is the goat's head."

I jumped to my feet. "Okay, this is ridiculous! Kids draw all sorts of things.... Sometimes they're moons. Sometimes they're flowers. And sometimes they're..."

"...Sigil of Baphomets?" completed Detective Zanderhoff.

"I think the plural is Sigils of Baphomet," corrected Officer Gallagher.

"Mr. Bolton, I can see you're upset," said Principal Hardly. "And you know I try to run a school where the children feel free to explore and express themselves. But I have to draw the line at Devil worship."

"Are you familiar with someone called The Dark Priest?" pressed Zanderhoff.

"Oh, please," I responded. "No. I do not know anyone named The Dark Priest."

"Are you a member of any Satanic organizations, Mr. Bolton?"

"No. I… Oh, this is just absurd!" I said as I marched over to the door and opened it. "Davin, can you come in here please?"

Davin hopped off the bench and marched into the Principal's office.

"Am I in trouble, Daddy?"

"No, Davin. You most definitely are not. Can you please tell these nice people what you were drawing?"

"Stars. Five stars."

"See?" I said in the most chastising tone I could muster.

"But Miss Catugno pulled it away before I could draw the goat's head."

CHAPTER NINE

LALLY MAKES A POINT

A Sigil of Baphomet is the official insignia of the Church of Satan. It generally consists of a downward-pointing star with a goat's head drawn inside. According to Wikipedia, it can't be reproduced without the express written permission from the Church of Satan. So not only was my little boy accused of a hate crime, Miss Catugno apparently prevented him from violating copyright laws, too.

The big question, of course, is how did Davin even know to draw such a thing? I'd never even heard of a Sigil of Baphomet. Naturally, Detective Zanderhoff wanted me to explain where Davin picked it up, but I honestly hadn't a clue. He pressed me with questions, coming just short of calling me and my family a coven of Devil worshippers.

Amazingly, I was able to calm everyone down. I assured them we were not witches and that Davin must have seen it in a comic book or something. I promised Principal Hardly that Davin and I would have a "little talk" and there would be no further problems in the Satanic Ritual Department. Principal Hardly looked skeptical, and Gallagher kept tapping his billyclub, looking like he wanted to Taser both of us. But Zanderhoff couldn't help but notice how cute little Davin was with his Thomas the Tank Engine backpack, and decided to cut us some slack.

As we were heading for the door, Zanderhoff warned us, "No more Satan stuff, you hear me little boy?"

"He doesn't like that name," said Davin.

I whisked Davin away before any additional questions could be asked.

As we drove home, I made a point of treating the entire matter lightly. It must've been a traumatic experience for Davin, who had never caused any trouble at the school before. Sitting on the office bench with the Principal and policemen parading in and out must have scared the little fella. So there was no mention of Dark Priests or Sigils of Basophets in my Honda Civic. We even stopped at Carvel for some ice cream, which cheered him right up. But as he licked his chocolate cone with rainbow sprinkles, I made up my mind that I would have to get to the bottom of this. Something strange was going on and I had to find out what it was.

When Lally got home from school, I said, "Lally, can I talk to you a minute?"

"It wasn't my fault," she blurted.

"I want to talk about Davin."

"Oh," she said, relieved. "What about him?"

"Wait. *What* wasn't your fault?"

"Oh, nothing. It's just something we teens say sometimes, like *What's up?*, *How's it hangin'*? *It wasn't my fault*. You know, that sort of thing."

It's amazing how our children think we're total idiots. But whatever "wasn't her fault" could not be as pressing as Davin's situation, so I let it drop.

I showed Lally Davin's artwork. "Davin drew this in kindergarten today."

She took the sheet from me and said, "Oh, cool. A Sigil of Baphomet!"

I was speechless.

"Without the goat's head."

"Right," said I. "I need to talk to you about stuff like this. Do you have any idea what's wrong with Davin?"

"Yeah, he's a little twerp."

"Stop it. Where is he getting all these Satan and Hell ideas from?"

"I don't know, Pop. Why don't you ask Carl the Boogeyman. LOL."

"Stop it, Lally. This is serious. There were policemen at his school over this drawing. Did you teach him about it?"

"Hey, it wasn't my fault."

"Is that a greeting like *How's it hangin'*? or are you really saying it wasn't your fault?"

Lally gave me a rare look. I think she had a glimmer of recognition that Daddy wasn't a total moron.

"I never talk to him about stuff like that, Dad. Why would I? It's creepy."

"Well," I asked, "is he playing any video games or watching any TV shows that deal with Satanism?"

"Wait! There was this episode of Dora The Explorer where she and Diego perform a blood ritual on Swiper the Fox," she exclaimed. "ROTFL!"

"Will you stop it with the texting acronyms. Be serious."

"How can I? You're saying my kid brother is a Devil worshiper," she rebutted.

"I am not," I insisted, but wondering at the same time if that wasn't exactly what I was doing. "It's just that he's getting these ideas from somewhere."

"Jeez, Pop. Sometimes I think you're dumber than Walter. Why don't you just ask Davin where he's getting this stuff from?"

"Don't talk that way about your mom's husband," I scalded, though I totally agreed with her. And of course Lally was 100% right about Davin, too. I had to have a serious talk with my son.

CHAPTER TEN

OF COURSE I BELIEVE YOU

*A*nd the boy said, "But there really was a wolf here! And now the flock has scattered! I cried out, 'Wolf! Wolf!' Why didn't anybody come to help me?" The old man tried to comfort the boy as they walked back to the village. "Nobody believes a liar," he said, putting his arm around the youth, "not even when he is telling the truth!"

Davin yawned, and I could see that he was almost ready to fall to sleep. As I put down the storybook, I decided this was as good a time as any to calmly ask him about all the strange things that were going on.

"Davin, do you know why nobody listened to the boy when he saw a wolf?" I asked.

"Because he made it up before so nobody believed him now," said Davin with a proud grin.

"Exactly, D. It's fun to make things up, but when you really want people to believe you, then it can cause trouble."

"If I ever see a wolf, will you believe me, Daddy?" he asked earnestly.

"Of course I will, Davin. But if you're making things

up, then you have to tell me they are made up so I won't worry. Okay?"

"Okay."

"Like the story you told me about how you met Satan."

"Lucifer," he corrected. "He doesn't…"

"He doesn't like the name Satan. Right. You told me. That's just the sort of thing I'm talking about, Davin. You made it up, but you're talking about it like it's real."

Davin sat up in bed, the sleepiness gone from his brown eyes. "But I didn't make it up, Daddy. I really really saw Lucifer."

I knew he was just a little kid, but I couldn't help but get a bit angry. "Stop it, Davin. Maybe you saw him on TV or in a book, but you didn't meet him."

"How do *you* know? You weren't there. You were walking around the hospital fighting with the doctors. You didn't see."

I froze. Davin was in a coma. He had no idea what I was doing.

"Lucifer even showed me the email you wrote. And he….
"

"He *what*?" I managed to stammer out.

"I wasn't supposed to tell you," he said sheepishly.

"Davin!" I said in a firm tone. "What did Lucifer do?"

"He laughed and then messed up your email. He said he does stuff like that all the time."

My head spun. I had never mentioned that email to Davin – the boy's only 6, for crying out loud. Yet not only did he know about the email, he knew that it had changed into some ridiculous piece of SPAM.

"How do you know about all that, Davin?" I asked in a stunned whisper.

"I told you. Lucifer showed me. He..." Davin's face scrunched up, which is something he does when he's trying hard to remember something. "Lucifer said he was... hashing into your email."

"Do you mean *hacking*?"

"Yeah! Hacking. That's it!"

I reeled. I tried very hard to keep my voice calm as I asked a question that I already knew the answer to.

"Where, Davin? Where did Sata... Lucifer show you all this?"

"In Hell, Daddy. When I got sick and went to Hell."

I let out a deep sigh. There were so many more questions I wanted to ask. But, frankly, I had all I could take for one day.

"Okay, kiddo. I think it's time to go to sleep now."

"You believe me, right Daddy?" he asked pleadingly.

"Yes, son," I said. It wasn't a total lie – I believed that Davin believed what he was saying.

"And if I tell you there's a wolf in the forest, you'll still believe me?"

"Yes, Davin, I'll always believe you," I said, giving him a kiss on the forehead while tucking the Transformers quilt around him.

"So," he continued, "you'll believe me that Carl is in the closet right now?"

CHAPTER ELEVEN
IS IT POSSIBLE?

I must confess, I blanked for a good five seconds. But then I realized what Davin was talking about.

"Carl the Boogeyman?" I asked.

Davin nodded sweetly.

"So the Boogeyman came to see you, Davin. Is that what you're saying?"

"No, Daddy. He came to see *you*. He said he had a message."

"What's the message, Davin?" I was beginning to lose my patience.

"Ask him yourself," he said with a shrug, then pointed toward the closet.

"Davin....." but what could I do but sigh? "I've really had enough of this," I said as I marched over to the closet door.

But when I placed my hand on the doorknob, I froze. For some unexplainable reason, a ripple of fear ran up my legs and through my spine. All the unanswered questions of the past few weeks raced through my brain – Davin's strange stories, the pentagrams in art class, the fact that Davin knew about things like the strange email. *Is it possible?* I asked myself for the first time.

But no. It simply was NOT possible. I was getting caught up in Davin's own over-active imagination. I took a deep breath, twisted the doorknob, and swung the closet door open wide.

"Is he still there, Daddy?" asked Davin from across the darkened room.

"No, son. He's not," I said. "But he left his banjo."

CHAPTER TWELVE
THE BANJO FROM HELL

I didn't sleep much that night. And it wasn't just the unanswered questions either. It wasn't Davin's strange behavior. It wasn't even the mysterious banjo that I found in his bedroom closet. Oh sure, any one of those things was enough to give any normal father the willies. But the thing that got to me the most was the message.

Scrawled on the drum of the banjo were three circles, and inside each circle was a word in a language I had never seen before. Perhaps nobody had. And the strange, angular letters were written in a red, clumpy liquid that could only be one thing – human blood. (Actually, it could have been many things. But given the rest of this creepy day, there was no reason to think it was anything but human blood.)

As the rest of my family slept the sweet sleep of the innocent, I sat by the fireplace studying the Banjo From Hell.

If that's what it was, of course. I mean, anyone could take a banjo and scrawl some demonic runes on it in human blood. I would imagine things like that happen in Nashville all the time. But how did it find its way into Davin's bedroom closet?

And, as if things weren't weird enough, Davin said one

more thing before I left his room with the banjo. Here are his exact words: "Oh, Daddy, Carl says it *was* Lally's fault."

This stopped me cold. "What was Lally's fault, Davin?"

"I don't know. He said you should check her sock drawer," said Davin, sleepily.

Check her sock drawer? I repeated to myself as I quietly closed Davin's door.

I know this is a crappy thing for an open-minded father to do, but while everyone slept, I snuck into Lally's room with a penlight and looked in her sock drawer. I didn't know what I was looking for or what I would say if my daughter woke up (and least is wasn't her panty drawer). I was about to dismiss the entire thing as nonsense, when my hand felt a Ziploc bag at the very rear of the drawer. Removing it, I discovered it was half filled with marijuana, along with a packet of EZ-Wider rolling papers and a disposable Bic lighter.

To tell you the truth, part of me was relieved. Considering what else had gone on today, I thought I might discover a severed foot or something. (Looking back, it was silly of me to think that. The severed foot wouldn't show up until much later.)

So there I sat by the fire, with the Banjo From Hell on my knee and a bag of my daughter's pot on the coffee table. There had to be a rational explanation for all of this – one that didn't involve trips to Hell and a banjo-playing Boogeyman named Carl. As I sat there late into the evening, I decided to do two things.

First – I was convinced I couldn't do this on my own. I resolved to seek out help from someone with experience in this field.

Second – As I stared at the banjo and marijuana, I decided on something I could do. No, I couldn't play the banjo, but...

CHAPTER THIRTEEN

THOSE DAMN DORITOS

After many hours of contemplation and three bags of Zesty Taco Doritos, I made the decision to seek out spiritual guidance. Did I believe Davin's story? Well, honestly, I didn't know what to believe at this point. The role of religion is to explain the unexplainable – and there was so much to this story I simply couldn't explain no matter how much I tried. Perhaps the Church could help.

My community has two Roman Catholic churches – St. Blaise of Carinola and St. Hyacinth's Basilica. In the end, my decision to go with Saint Blaise was purely whimsical in nature.

Oh, Saint Hyacinth was by no means a slouch. In the year 1214, when his monastery was under attack by barbaric Tartarians, the Virgin Mary spoke to him and requested he save her statue from the savages. Though the statue weighed nearly a ton, Hyacinth miraculously carried it away as if it were weightless. There's a good number of churches throughout the world baring the name of Saint Hyacinth, as well as a handful of health clubs.

But Saint Blaise's story struck me as more dramatic and compelling. Way back in 316 A.D., Bishop Blaise was a fugitive who had dared to break the law against praying.

He went into hiding in a cave, where he found himself surrounded by wild animals. The praying must have paid off, because they all became the best of friends. Eventually though, poor Blaise was found and ordered to stand trial. Just before the trial, however, Blaise performed a miracle before the astonished townspeople – he persuaded a wolf to return an elderly woman's stolen pig. Despite this miracle, however, the Governor had Blaise skinned alive and then beheaded. If it were me, I think I would have preferred the opposite order.

So I chose St. Blaise of Carinola as the place to seek spiritual guidance.

But before I went there, I had the little matter of Lally's stash to deal with. Lally must have sensed something was up, because she made a mad dash for the door as soon as she'd gotten dressed. But I blocked her path.

"Hi, Dad. Gotta go. Late for school," she said, trying to sound chipper.

I was in no mood for games. "What wasn't your fault?"

"I…"

"It's not a greeting like *What's happenin.* What happened that you don't want to be blamed for?"

I could see her brain racing with questions like, *How did he find out? What does he know? Does this have anything to do with my missing pot?*

I decided to put her out of her misery and held up the Ziploc bag.

"Oh, shit," she said.

"Yes. Oh, shit," I concurred. "What happened?"

"Nancy Langworthy got busted at school for smoking pot behind the bleachers," she blurted.

"So what does that have to do with you?" was my obvious follow-up question.

She took a deep breath. "I gave her the joint. She swore to me she didn't tell anyone. Damn! How'd you find out?"

I've always made it a policy not to lie to my children. But what was I going to say – "Carl the Boogeyman told me?" After giving it a moment's thought, I realized that it was indeed the perfect response.

"Carl the Boogeyman told me," I said, looking her right in the eye.

"Okay, don't tell me," she said, turning to walk out.

"Not so fast, Miss Pothead. You're grounded for a month."

"Geez, Dad," she moaned. Then she had a wicked look in her eye. "I noticed you polished off the Doritos last night," she said knowingly.

"Okay. Two weeks. Now get outta here."

CHAPTER FOURTEEN
PERFECTLY GOOD PIG

St. Blaise's was located in one of the nicer sections of town, situated on a tree-lined street among gently rolling hills. I'd passed it a thousand times, noticing the signs for bake sales, turkey raffles, or their annual St. Blaise's Feast – a popular event that included food stands, kiddy rides, and more spiritual activities such as roulette and blackjack.

Since it was late morning, the parking lot was nearly empty. I parked the Honda by the front entrance, took the Banjo From Hell out of the back, and entered St. Blaise's.

It was very quiet inside. The only person in sight was an elderly lady in the front pew, praying to a relief carving that depicted Saint Blaise convincing the wolf to release the pig. I walked up to the woman and asked, "Excuse me, do you know where I can find a Priest?"

"I think the real hero of the story is the wolf," she said, without turning to face me.

"Excuse me?"

"He had the pig, you understand." Now she turned to me with pleading eyes. "The wolf had the pig and he agreed to let it go just to save Saint Blaise. So you tell me –

Who's the real hero of the story, eh?"

"The wolf?"

"Bingo!" she exclaimed.

Then I made the mistake of asking a follow-up question. "So why are you praying to St. Blaise?"

"I'm not. I'm praying to the wolf."

"Ah!" I said, in an exaggerated tone of understanding. The woman was clearly a nutcase. "Do you know where I can find a priest?" I tried again.

Her bones actually creaked as she stood up. "I think Father Ryan is on confessional duty. It's over yonder, Jed Clampett," she cackled.

It took me a moment to realize she was referring to my banjo.

"Thank you," I said as I walked toward the confessional.

"The wolf should be the real saint," she called after me. "Perfectly good pig!"

For a relatively modern church, the confessional was quite elaborate. It was made out of oak or mahogany and intricately carved. I swung open the lattice work door and stepped inside. It was dark and musty, with a faint hint of Master XK-12 – the stuff they spray in rental bowling shoes when you return them.

Behind a small screen, a wood panel slid aside. It was dark on the other side as well, and I could only make out

Father Ryan's silhouette.

"May the Lord be in your heart to help you make a good confession, my son," said the silhouette.

"Thank you, Father," I replied. "I'm actually not here to confess."

"Oh, that's too bad," he replied. "You look like you'd have some real doozies."

"I need to ask some advice."

"You sure? No cheating on the spouse? Maybe some lap dances on the way home from work?"

"Sorry."

"Everybody's got something," he insisted. "Come on, give it a shot."

"Then can I ask my question?"

"Anything you want," he chirped.

I took a deep breath and tried to recall how this worked. "Bless me, Father, for I have sinned."

"That's my boy," he beamed.

"It has been, oh I don't know, 23 years since my last confession."

"Whoa, Nelly!"

"Uh, let's see…. I think my ex-wife's husband is a doofus."

"Is he?"

"Oh, yeah. Big time."

"Then it's not a sin. Hit me again."

"Uh, last month, at the McDonald's drive-thru, I handed the girl a ten and she gave me back change for a twenty."

"I see. And you failed to tell her about her error?"

"I considered it," I admitted. "But there were cars behind me and, well, I just drove away and pocketed the extra money."

"I see," he sighed, clearly disappointed. "Anything…" Father Ryan paused. I'm certain he wanted to say "better" or "juicier." "Anything else?"

I decided to throw the poor guy a bone.

"Last night I smoked some of my daughter's marijuana."

"Now that's more like it!" he exploded. The confessional actually shook.

"Can I ask my question now?"

"For your act of contrition," he said, ignoring me, "I want you to go back to McDonald's and return the stolen ten dollars. Then I want you to get the marijuana and bring it to me where I can dispose of it properly."

"Father...."

"Do you want me to answer your questions or not?" I shut up. "Also say five Hail Mary's and two Our Father's. Now what's your question?"

"It concerns this," I said, holding up the Banjo From Hell to the screen.

Father Ryan brought his face closer to the screen and his eyes opened wide. "Jesus Mary Joseph!" he exclaimed.

"You recognize it?" I asked hopefully.

"I do. I do indeed!" he said, and I think he crossed himself. "Do you have any idea what you have there?"

"No. That's why I'm here. What is it?!"

"You don't know? Good God, man! It's a Gibson Florentine Vox-4! You know what those things go for?"

I realized he was talking about the banjo.

"Hold on!" he said, and I could hear him rummaging around for something. To my astonishment, harmonica music came from the other side of the screen. "Let's jam, son!"

The Priest began playing a fairly decent rendition of "Oh, Susannah."

"Wait!" I cried, bringing the music to a halt. "I can't play this thing."

"Oh, of course you can't. There's not enough room. Come on, let's go up to the apse – the acoustics are killer back there."

Without waiting for an answer, he closed the wood panel separating us and stepped out of the confessional. I had no choice but to follow with my Gibson Florentine Vox-4.

"Father, please. Listen to me," I pleaded. "I don't play the banjo. It arrived at my house under mysterious circumstances and I thought maybe the Church could help."

"Oh," said Ryan, pocketing the harmonica. "Well, I'm not sure I can help you with a banjo."

"It's not the banjo," I explained. "It's what is written on it. It's this…" I held it up so the strange writing was clearly visible to him.

For a brief moment, it appeared as if the scrawls were meaningless to him. But then he backed away, pale as a ghost and screamed! He ran to the marble Baptistery and dunked his entire head under the Holy Water. He remained there far longer than I would have thought possible.

I followed him and tapped him on the shoulder, concerned he might drown. He finally resurfaced, gasping for breath.

"Father, what is it?" I asked. "Do you know what it says?"

"Return the money," he said between gasps.

"What money?"

"The McDonald's money. Keep the pot. I don't want it. Say 15,433 Hail Mary's…. No 15,434. The two Our Fathers should still be fine. Now take that abomination out of here," he commanded then hurried away.

"But what does it mean?" I begged.

But Father Ryan didn't answer. He disappeared through a door behind the altar.

Clutching my Gibson Florentine Vox-4, I stood there in the church at a total loss.

"Bring it here," said a woman's voice. Looking up, I saw it was the old crone I spoke with earlier. "Lemme take a look at it."

Having nothing to lose, I brought the banjo over the woman. She removed an old pair of Pince-nez from her purse and put them on. She studied the runes just a moment before saying, "Yep. Pretty much what I figured."

"What does it mean?"

"Not sure, sonny. Not sure," she said, clearly puzzled. "But this ain't the type of church that's gonna help you."

Maybe I was just dense. "What kind of church would know?"

"Oh, you can figure that one out," she said with a wink, and returned to her praying.

What could I do? I tucked the Gibson Florentine Vox-4 under my arm and headed for the exit. As I stepped into the vestibule, I heard the old lady call out to me…

"Be careful, sonny. That's a powerful instrument you got there." And then, just before I stepped out into the parking, she said, "And that's not Carl's handwriting."

I froze momentarily, than dashed back into the Church... But nobody was there. It might have been my imagination, but I could almost make out someone saying, "perfectly good pig."

CHAPTER FIFTEEN

THE BLOCKS! THE BLOCKS!

When the caller ID indicated it was the school calling, an overwhelming wave of despair swept over me. "Not again," I moaned as I pressed "Talk."

"Hello?"

"Mr. Bolton. It's Principal Hardly. There's been another…. Well, I don't know what to call it."

"Is Davin…"

"Don't worry. The police aren't involved. At least not yet."

I was going to ask "Is Davin okay?" But it was good news that Davin wasn't under schoolhouse arrest this time. I dreaded the thought of dealing with Detective Zanderhoff again.

"Should I come over?" I asked.

"Right away," he replied. "Uh, Mr. Bolton, do you speak Latin in your household?"

"No. I remember a little French from high school. Why?"

"Get over here," he ordered, and hung up the phone.

As I pulled up to Old Bethpage Elementary School, I saw Principal Hardly waiting for me out in front. He wasn't beet red this time, so perhaps the situation wasn't so dire. Or maybe he was on medication. After learning the problem, I decided it was the latter.

"Please, come with me," he said hurriedly. "You need to see this before anyone messes it up."

"Messes *what up*?"

"The blocks, Mr. Bolton. The wooden blocks."

Without any further explanation, he pulled me into the school and rushed me down a hallway.

My son's kindergarten teacher is a sweet, elderly woman named Mrs. Huvey. She'd worked at Old Bethpage Elementary since the day it opened, and could have retired long ago had she chosen to. I considered Davin lucky to have her as his teacher.

We entered the classroom to find that only Mrs. Huvey and Davin were present.

"Hi, Daddy. Am I in trouble again?" asked Davin.

"I don't think so, champ, but let's find out," I said with an assuring wink.

"Thank you so much for coming, Mr. Bolton," said Mrs.

Huvey, sweetly. She turned to Davin, "I'm just gonna talk to Daddy a minute, okay dumpling?" she said, tussling his hair.

She gently took my arm and guided me outside into the hallway.

"Mr. Bolton, your kid is seriously fucked up," she said in a harsh whisper.

"Excuse me?"

"I've been teaching for 52 years and I have never... NEVER... seen anything ... ANYTHING... like this."

"Anything like *what*?" I asked.

She stared me directly in the eyes as if drilling her thoughts into my brain. "The blocks, Mr. Bolton. The blocks." Then she turned back to her sweet, ol' self and said, "Let's go take a look, shall we?" Mrs. Huvey pivoted and strolled back into the classroom.

She led Principal Hardly and me over to an open section of floor. "This is our Choice Play Area, Mr. Bolton. I set aside part of each day for the children to play and express themselves in any way their little hearts desire. A practice I am ending as of today."

The floor was covered with those foam, interlocking squares that formed sort of a giant jigsaw puzzle. There were books, Tinker Toys, some opened cans of Play Doh... and then there were the blocks.

Blocks of the sort Mrs. Huvey had are common to nurseries, pre-schools, and kindergarten classes all across the country. They're made of wood, with different alphabet letters on each side. Usually, kids use them to spell out simple words such as "CAT", "BUG," or if the teacher isn't looking, "POOP." But in this instance, the blocks had been used for a slightly more sophisticated message.

They read…

Brevior saltare cum deformibus mulieribus est vita

"Davin did this?" I asked needlessly.

"Yep," said Mrs. Huvey, jamming that short syllable with as much scorn and sarcasm as she could muster.

"It looks like Latin."

"D-U-H," said Mrs. Huvey. An image of Lally and a bag of Doritos flashed through my brain.

"I don't speak Latin. Neither does Davin," I explained.

"Then we have a little problem, don't we?" said the elderly teacher.

"What's Latin?" asked Davin from his desk.

"Latin, my dear," answered Mrs. Huvey, "is a very, very, very old language. People really don't use it anymore. But when I was a little girl, they made us learn it."

"So you can read this?" I asked.

"Yes. I most certainly can."

"Well, what does it say?'

Rather than answer, she walked to the chalkboard and wrote "Brevior saltare cum deformibus mulieribus est vita" in impeccable handwriting. She pronounced each Latin word as she wrote it. Then, she turned her back to me and began writing something else. She clearly was going for the surprise factor, since her back blocked what she was writing. I could hear the chalk tapping and squeaking as it raced across the blackboard.

When she was finished, she stepped aside to reveal the translation:

Life is too short to dance with ugly women.

"Oh, this is absurd," I blurted. "You're telling me Davin wrote 'Life is too short to dance with ugly women'?"

"In Latin," said Principal Hardly and Mrs. Huvey in unison.

"Impossible," I insisted. My mind reeled for an explanation. "Have you considered that maybe it was just a random coincidence?"

Mrs. Huvey lowered her glasses and said, "Brevior saltare cum plumbeus vovo in dubium." I think it meant "Life's too short to answer stupid questions."

"Oh, we considered that, Mr. Bolton," injected Principal Hardly. "But the odds that those blocks might have fallen that way by chance are even greater than the odds of the Teacher's Union agreeing to give up tenure."

He shot Mrs. Huvey a critical look. Apparently there was some political backstory I wasn't privy to. Still, I got the point. There was no way this was just a bizarre accident.

I felt totally helpless. Yes, things were strange and there was no plausible explanation. But what was I supposed to do about it? I asked Principal Hardly that very question. "I understand your concern, but what am I supposed to do?"

He reached into the inner pocket of his sports coat and took out a business card. "I think it's time you made an appointment with Dr. Lapinsky."

"Is he a child psychologist?" I asked as I reached for the card.

Mrs. Huvey and Principal Hardly shared another look…. but this time they burst out laughing.

CHAPTER SIXTEEN
PRACTITIONER

Dr. Jonathan Lapinsky's office was located in nearby Huntington. The Town of Huntington is best known for its Heckscher Bottle Museum - one of the largest archives of glass beverage containers in the world. Its rare and valuable bottle collection has been valued at over $23 million, plus an additional $43 in deposits.

The card that Principal Hardly handed me was sort of sparse. Besides the address, the only thing written on the plain white card was:

Dr. Jonathan Lapinsky, Ph.D., D.D., D.D.A.
Practitioner

Practitioner of what? I asked myself more than once. As Davin and I sat in his waiting room, there was certainly no clue as to what he actually practitioned. In fact, it was perhaps the most generic doctor's office I'd ever visited. Old magazines rested on the end table. An Escher print adorned one wall – it was the one where a waterfall was impossibly feeding itself a continuous flow of water. There was an umbrella stand, an empty candy dish, and a sign that said "Please No Cell Phones." The only unusual item in the room was an aquarium. The fish were normal enough, but instead of the usual sunken pirate ship or deep-sea diver, there was a life-sized skeleton of a human foot. Davin and I watched as angelfish swam in and out between the toes. (At this point, you're probably supposing that the foot skeleton was real. Sadly, I never found out for certain.)

After a while, the inner door opened and an elderly man appeared in the doorway. He appeared to be in his 80s and wore a tunic made from some coarse, brown fabric. A large silver cross hung around his neck on a leather strap. His left foot was barefoot, and his right foot was, well, missing. An old-fashioned peg-leg took its place.

Davin reached the same conclusion that you probably have. He stared at the peg leg, gulped audibly, and then cast a furtive glance back toward the fish tank. I could practically hear the wheels in his head spinning. He began to ask the obvious question, "Is that…" but Dr. Lapinsky cut him off.

"Ahhhhh, this must be little Davin!" said the good doctor. "And Mr. Bolton. How nice to meet you both."

"Principal Hardly spoke very highly of you," I lied. Besides handing me the card and ordering us to get out, he hadn't said much at all.

"Principal Hardly?" he said, perplexed. Then, "Oh, Oscar! Yes, Oscar Hardly." He seemed to get lost in thought, recalling something. "Do you know if he ever got rid of them?"

"Got rid of what?" I asked.

"Ah, no matter," said Lapinsky with a dismissive wave of his hand. "Sometimes they vanish. And sometimes they stick around for the rest of your life… and then some. Am I right? Come in, come in," he said without any further explanation.

Davin looked at me. Understandably, he seemed a bit frightened.

"It'll be fine, chief," I assured him, hoping I was telling the truth.

I took Davin's hand and led him into Dr. Lapinsky's... well, "office" is not really the proper word. Traditionally, offices have desks and chairs, bookshelves, windows – that sort of stuff. Dr. Lapinsky's room looked more like a maharaja's tent. If there were actual walls and a ceiling, they weren't in view. There were no chairs, just decorative pillows strewn around a circular rug. The largest item in the tent was a large, intricately decorated pirate's chest. Had it been much, much smaller, it would have looked perfect at the bottom of that fish tank instead of the foot skeleton.

"I need to go to the potty," said Davin meekly.

"Sure you do!" replied Lapinksy. "Please, everyone make yourself comfortable. Have a seat."

Davin looked at me. I shrugged and plopped myself down on a cushion with the cartoon character Ziggy embroidered on it. Davin sat down right next to me.

"Let's begin by cleansing the air, shall we?" said Lapinsky. He opened the trunk and took out a can of Master KX-12 and sprayed it around. "This stuff's remarkable. They market it for bowling alleys, but we know what it really does, don't we?" He winked at Davin, who moved even closer to me.

"Dr. Lapinsky, I gotta tell you, I'm not even sure why we're here," I confessed. "Principal Hardly suggested it was a good idea."

"He's a smart man. Insightful. I'm sure you did the right thing."

"Davin's always been perfectly fine. We've never had need of a psychologist before," I told him.

"Psychologist? Heaven's, where did you get that idea? I'm no psychologist."

"Then what are you? What's your profession?"

"I'm an exorcist. Is anyone thirsty? There's some Vitamin Water in the chest."

"An exorcist?!" I sprang to my feet. "Are you kidding me?"

"Don't worry. I'm dully licensed and accredited. In fact, if you work for the state, your insurance covers it."

"This is crazy," I insisted.

"No really. You'd be amazed how many civil servants are possessed. Show me a Post Office or a D.M.V. and I'll show you at least one lost soul being controlled by dark spirits."

"Daddy, what's an exorcist?" asked Davin.

"Um, uh…" I didn't know how to begin to explain that to a 6 year old. But Mr. Lapinsky saved me the trouble.

"Little boy," he began, "There are all sorts of powers in the universe. There are good powers and there are bad powers. Sometimes good powers guide us and help us do wonderful things."

"Like when I kicked that winning soccer goal?" he asked.

"Exactly like that. But sometimes bad powers want in on the fun, too. Sometimes they get deep down inside us and make us do all sorts of things we don't want to do."

Davin nodded. "What sort of things?" he asked.

And then Lapinsky's delicate explanation took an unexpectedly gruesome turn. "Things like THIS, lad!" he bellowed, and waved his peg leg inches from Davin's nose.

"They made you cut off your foot?!" asked Davin in horror.

"No. That was a snowmobile accident. But they made me get this wooden job instead of a realistic prosthesis. Those fiends."

I'd had enough of this nonsense. "Thank you for your time, Dr. Lapinsky. But my son is not possessed."

"You know how you sound, Mr. Bolton? Like a man who's trying to convince himself of something he doesn't believe in his heart," said Lapinsky, lifting a line straight out of Casablanca. "Strange things have been happening, am I correct? Things that have no possible explanation."

"I'm sorry. My boy is perfectly normal," I repeated. "Come on, Davin. Let's go."

Lapinsky sighed, then held out his hands in the universal gesture of resignation. Then he said, "*Mandus vult decipi...*"

And Davin said, "*…ergo decipiatur.*"

Lapinsky and I stared at Davin in amazement. "What?" asked Davin. "Did I say a bad word like Lally uses?"

For the second time that day I was asked, "Do you speak Latin in your household, Mr. Bolton?"

"No. What did he say?"

"I said 'The world wants to be deceived' and your son finished the phrase 'so let it be deceived.'"

"Yeah, Lucifer said it while he was letting me feed the hounds."

"Like I said, my boy is perfectly normal," I said. "I mean, for a boy who's fed the Hounds of Hell."

CHAPTER SEVENTEEN
ONIARAK B'SHABA

So I told Lapinsky The Exorcist the entire story.

[AUTHOR'S NOTE: At this point in my original manuscript, I had written a two-page recap of everything that had transpired up until now. Though I thought (and still think) it was necessary, my infernal editor claimed it slowed down the narrative and insisted I take it out. If you experience any bouts of confusion, please email him at editor@hellisforreal.com and perhaps we can re-instate it in a future edition.]

Dr. Lapinsky sat impassively while I told him the ordeal Davin and I had been through. Occasionally he jotted down a few notes on a legal pad, and once stopped me to ask the exact flavor of Doritos I'd eaten the night I found the banjo. He scribbled down "Zesty Taco," underlined it, then had me continue.

Once I was finished, he sat motionless, hand on his chin in deep concentration. While he pondered, I took Davin to use the potty off the waiting room. Thankfully, there was absolutely nothing weird or macabre about the bathroom. Everything was totally normal, right down to the "Don't Flush Paper Towels" message written in Sharpie on a sheet of copy paper.

When we returned to the tent, Lapinsky was gone. In his place – in fact, in the same pensive position that we had left Lapinsky in – sat the old crone from St. Blaise's Church. (Had the editor let me recap, you'd know immediately who I was talking about. She's the old woman who said "perfectly good pig.")

"What are you doing here?" I asked. "And where's Dr. Lapinsky?"

The old crone cackled. "He called in the big guns. You didn't flush any paper towels, did you?"

"No."

"Good. There should be a special place in Hell for plumbers that gouge. In fact, there is."

"Who is she, Daddy?" asked Davin, every bit as confused as I was.

"My name's notimportant," she said cavalierly. "Rita Notimportant," she clarified. (I bet you thought that was a typo.) "Let's just say that Dr. Lapinsky and I have a close working relationship. *Very* close."

Though Lapinsky was an oddball, I couldn't imagine she was making a sexual inference. I know it's crazy, but at that moment I was sure that Lapinsky and Notimportant were the same person. She watched me come to this conclusion and said, "Bingo!" as if she could read my mind.

She smiled sweetly, showing off her tooth, then bade us to sit. *"Toto, sentio nos in kansate non iam adesse,"* she chanted in Latin.

Reflexively, I turned to my 6-year-old son for the translation.

"Hey, don't look at me," he said.

She explained, "It means, 'Toto, I have a feeling we're not in Kansas anymore.' It's from an old movie."

"Yes, I might have seen it," I said flatly.

"You and your son have entered a new world. New to you, but quite old. Older, in fact, than the Earth itself, Mr. Bolton. May I call you Henry?"

"Sure," I said, though my name was Richard.

"Henry, it's understandable that you're confused. But I think I can tell you what's happening," she boasted.

"You really know?" I asked hopefully.

She nodded. "I need to see the pawn ticket again, please?"

"Huh?"

"Oh, I'm sorry. The banjo. I need to see the banjo again. Did you bring it?"

It was in the trunk of my car, so Davin and I ran outside to get it. Fortunately, when we returned, Rita Notimportant hadn't morphed into Carrot Top or anybody else. I handed her the Gibson Florentine Vox-4 and waited while she examined it. She was quiet at first, but then she began nodding and chortling as she studied the strange symbols on the white drum of the banjo.

"Ahh, Lucifer, you're a tricky S.O.B." she cackled. "It was the three circles that threw me off."

"What about them? What do they mean?"

"The circles aren't letters at all," she announced "They're an ancient symbol that's still used to this very day."

Great. A minute ago I was Dorothy in The Wizard of Oz. Now I was Robert Langon in The DaVinci Code. "Will you please just tell us what it says?"

"No one appreciates a suspenseful moment any more," she said and spat. "It's a pawn ticket. The three circles are the Medici Orbs – a symbol for pawn shops since the Middle Ages."

I decided to play along. "Okay, the banjo is a pawn ticket. A pawn ticket for what?"

"Ahhh, finally an intelligent question, Henry," she said in all seriousness.

"What's a pawn ticket?" asked Davin, not wanting to be left out of this crucial discovery.

So I told him what a pawn shop was and how pawn tickets function. "When people leave things of value behind in a pawn shop, they're given a ticket so they can get it back later. But they have to pay the price before the pawn broker will let it go."

"But I didn't pawn anything," said Davin sadly.

"Perhaps you did, young man," said the old crone.

"Perhaps you did. Let's look at the words inside the balls." She pointed to the first circle and the strange symbol within. "This is Aramaic, a language over three thousand years old."

"You learned Aramaic? When?" I asked.

"Let's just say we didn't have iPads back then," she snickered. "The word in the first circle is *T'sod*, which means holding or captured." She pointed to the second circle. "The middle circle says *oniarak*. This is an adjective meaning *very long*. As in the sentence, 'The Captain of the Guard has a *oniarak b'shaba*.'"

"What's that mean?" asked Davin innocently.

"Just go on," I insisted.

"The final circle contains the word *B'Tsaoreh*. This is Aramaic for the English word *neck*," she concluded, clearly proud of herself.

"So the banjo is a pawn ticket with *holding long neck* written on it," I said incredulously.

"More or less," replied the crone.

"But that's meaningless!" I exclaimed.

"No it's not," shouted Davin. "*Long neck* is for a giraffe. They're holding Mr. Peety prisoner!"

"Bingo!" she yelled for the umpteenth time. "Such a smart boy," she remarked as she tossed Davin a sucking candy.

"Hold on a minute! Are you saying my son's toy giraffe is being held captive down in Hell?" I asked, clearly the most absurd question to ever leave my lips.

"Exactly," she replied. "To get Mr. Peety back you have to bring the pawn ticket and pay the price."

"Okay, I'll play along. Assuming I'm on board for all this, there's still something we're overlooking."

"What, Daddy?" asked Davin.

"Yeah, Daddy, what?" echoed the crone, in a tone that sort of annoyed me.

"Well," I began, "let's say some guy pawns a bracelet. When he leaves the bracelet at the pawnshop, the pawnbroker gives him money for it. When he repays the money, he gets the bracelet back. Right?"

"That's how it works," she answered, unwrapping a sucking candy for herself.

"But if they really kept Mr. Peety, what thing of value did they give Davin?" Even as I asked the question, I knew the answer.

So did Davin. "Lucifer let me go home, Daddy."

"Bingo!" Notimportant threw him another candy.

"Will you stop that!" I cried. "He's not a sea lion."

Davin laughed and made "ooop, ooop" noises while clapping his hands.

I took a deep breath and stood up. "Well, okay then. I got my boy back, they got Mr. Peety. Happy ending."

"It is not!!!!!" screamed Davin. "It is not! It's not a happy ending at all! We can't leave Mr. Peety down there!"

"I'll buy you another one."

"No! No! No!" he cried.

"Your daddy's not as smart as you are, little one," she cackled, and turned to me. "It's not that simple, Mr. Bolton. Strange things are happening with Davin, and they're going to keep happening and get worse until you pay Lucifer back for releasing him. You can buy your son a thousand Mr. Peety's and life still won't get back to normal."

"This is insane. What am I supposed to do? Pay Satan? How do I do that? And how much?"

"There's only one currency Satan craves. Human souls," she explained.

Her intense stare shut me up like a faucet. Did Satan want me in Davin's place? Is that what all this was about? Was I supposed to sacrifice my soul for my boy? Certainly, I would do it if I had to, but…

"Satan doesn't want you, dummy," said Notimportant, reading my thoughts. "At least I don't believe so. But there's something he does want, and your life's gonna be a mess until you figure out what it is."

"But how can I do that?" I pleaded. "How can I possibly know what Satan wants?"

"I know one way, but your not gonna like it," she told me.

"What?" I asked sarcastically. "I'm supposed to go to Hell and ask him?"

"Bingo!"

CHAPTER EIGHTEEN

SURFING FOR SATAN

I know I was doing it to save my boy, but the prospect of actually going to Hell scared the bejeezes out of me. I've always had a phobia about traveling to distant places. When I was a kid, my parents put me on a bus and said I was just going to an amusement park for the afternoon. It turns out they were shipping me to Camp Tonkahona, a sleep-away camp that held me hostage for 8 weeks. In hindsight, I should have seen it coming. I mean, why should I need a steamer trunk for a day at an amusement park? Both my parents are nearing retirement now. One day soon, I'm gonna say we're going to TGI Fridays, then dump them both in an old folks' home. Kumbaya that, Mom and Dad.

Ever since that Camp Tonkahona stunt, I've had an aversion to travel. Oh, I've made the pilgrimage to Disney World with the family and backpacked through Europe during college, but that's about it. So even if Hell wasn't, well, Hell, the thought of going there still freaked me out a little.

But how do you get to Hell? Sure, the Bible is full of ways, but each one of them includes the little matter of dying first. I'd asked Rita Notimportant, but she insisted she couldn't help me in that department. Like Dorothy in the Wizard of Oz, it was one of those things I would have to discover for myself, she insisted. I didn't own any ruby slippers, so I had to find another way.

This may sound ridiculous, but since I use the Internet for everything else, I thought the Web might help me get to Hell, too. I booted up my Dell and logged on.

"Ok, Henry," I said to myself with a chuckle. "Where shall we begin?"

Since I wanted to go somewhere, I decided to begin at a travel site. I chose Priceline.com for a number reasons. First, if by some chance they could find me safe passage to Hell, I would be able to name my own price. Second, I also had a sneaking suspicion that William Shatner himself had made some form of pact with the Devil. I could think of no other explanation for his amazingly successful career.

So I went to Priceline.com and entered "Hell" as my destination. The results were not very encouraging. Captain Kirk was able to offer me trips to Hella, Iceland; Helland, United Kingdom; Hellenthal, Germany; Hellin, Spain; Hellingly, United Kingdom; Hellevoetsluis and Hellendoom, Netherlands. I actually thought the name "Hellendoom" was pretty cool and saved it as a last resort.

I had slightly better luck with Hotwire.com. They were able to offer me a flight to Vaernes, Norway, which was just a few miles away from an actual town named Hell. The town is most famous for producing Mona Grudt, Miss Universe 1990, who billed herself as "The Beauty Queen From Hell." (I must confess, I took a little web-surfing detour and spent a good fifteen minutes looking at photographs of Miss Grudt.)

I put my libido in check and plowed on.

TripAdvisor.com also came back with Hell, Norway,

but took the extra step of offering me a suite in the Rica Hell Hotel. According to TripAdvisor, it is the #1 Rated Hotel in Hell. But before you go booking a room, you should know it's also the only hotel in Hell.

None of these destinations seemed promising, and I quickly determined that travel sites were not the way to go about it.

Davin's unfinished Sigil of Baphomet still sat on my desk, and I recalled it was copyrighted by the Church of Satan. On a whim, I typed churchofsatan.com into the Firefox address bar and…. Sure enough! The welcome screen for the Official Website of the Church of Satan filled my screen. I found myself looking at a man in a tacky Devil costume and fake horns. He was brandishing an ornate sword while surrounded by people in Pagan animal masks.

At first I thought I'd hit pay dirt, but then reality set in. I happened to have first-hand knowledge that Lucifer loathed the name Satan – so how connected could the Church of Satan really be? Besides, the website indicated they were based in a P.O. Box in the Grand Central Station Post Office, so I didn't have much confidence in them.

I began Googling all sorts of related terms – Devil worship, Hades, and Netherworld – but nothing came up that would be useful.

Then, on a whim, I Googled the entire phrase "don't call him Satan." The top result with that search term was for the website BrotherhoodOfLucifer.com. Now that sounded promising, so I clicked on it. To my disappointment, the dreaded "Page cannot be found" screen appeared on my monitor.

Once again, the entire message looked like this

> **Page cannot be found.**
> The page you are looking for might have been removed, had its name changed, or is temporarily unavailable.
> HTTP 666 – File not found

I was just about to click away and return to Google, when something caught my eye. I'd seen this same page a hundred times, and "HTTP 666 – File not found" just seemed odd somehow. On a whim, I clicked on the "666."

The dull webpage seemed to catch fire from the spot I clicked, and burned away into ash within seconds. This revealed a totally black screen with "BrotherhoodOfLucifer. com" displayed in flaming letters. Below that was the word "Password" and a white space for it to be typed in.

Naturally, I had no idea what the password was. And there was nothing else on the screen to help me. No "Contact Us" link, no "About Us" link, and certainly no "What's The Freakin' Password?" link. The mysterious and unfriendly nature of the webpage made me all the more confident that the people behind this might be the ones who could help me.

With nothing to lose, I decided to try guessing. First I typed in the word "password" and hit ENTER. I didn't expect it to work, and it didn't. A little smiley face with Devil horns appeared briefly along with a message "You have three more tries."

I thought to myself, "If I ran a Satanic website, what would I want as the password?" I typed in "Hail Lucifer" and waited. The Devil smiley appeared again along with the message, "Nice sentiment. You have two more tries."

My eyes roved around the room, looking for something to trigger an idea. Soon my attention focused on Davin's artwork. Bingo! I typed in "Sigil of Basophet" and hit ENTER. Once again, the Devil smiley popped up along with a new message: "The Church of Satan's for pussies. You have one more try."

Shit. I was down to my last attempt and I hadn't a clue. I thought back on the day's events, hoping something would trigger an epiphany. Did Lapinsky say something, anything, that would get me in? How about Notimportant? Maybe something in Aramaic or Latin? The whole day was a blur. In fact, only one thing the crone said echoed in my head.

Could it be?

I turned my attention back to the Password field and typed the word "Bingo."

There was a long moment where nothing happened (or perhaps it just seemed long). The little Devil appeared along with a message that completely caught me off guard. It read, "Henry, is that you?"

The page leaped to another page. At the top was "Welcome to the International Brotherhood of Lucifer Webpage." I've visited countless web sites over the years, and this one was as professional and stylish as the best of them. There were all the familiar links: About Us, Events, Contact Us, and so on. I was surprised to see a link for a demonic dating service called D-Date and even an online store. (I briefly checked it out. It offered such items as Freeze-Dried Ram's Blood and a t-shirt that read "My Grandpa went to Hell and all I got was this lousy t-shirt.")

Two links were of particular interest to me. The first

was "Frequently Asked Questions." This seemed like a superb place to begin, so I clicked it.

Brotherhood of Lucifer Frequently Asked Questions

1. Are you guys for real?

Yes. We are very much for real. We worship the Father of Lies, Prince of Darkness, or whatever other name you or Neil Gaiman drums up for him.

2. How do I join?

There are three easy steps. First, complete the PDF application below. Second, mail in your application along with payment for the level of membership you selected. Lastly, locate the Dagger of Aphenoff and, with it, make a sacrifice to Gog and Magog, then wait 6-8 weeks for delivery of your membership card.

3. Are you sure you're for real?

Hold on. We'll double check. Yes, we're for real.

4. If Lucifer is so evil, why do you want to be associated with him?

We checked out all the other major religions and the Devil just had so much more to offer. Plus, the chicks are really hot.

5. How do you get ox blood stains off upholstery?

Master KX-12.

666. My parents were Jewish, can I still become a member?

Unfortunately not. But you are more than welcome at our sister organization JewsForSatan.com. Tell them we sent you and get a free Heironomous Bosch yarmulke with each membership.

7. How do I get to Hell?

Of all the Frequently Asked Questions, this is the one least frequently asked. You enter through the Portal of Gugalanna.

I had never heard of the Portal of Gugalanna, and a subsequent Google search of the term yielded no results whatsoever. I did learn something about Gugalanna, though. He was a Sumerian Bull God who was slain and dismembered by Gilgamesh.

The second link of interest on the web page was "Find A Local Chapter." Clicking this link brought up another black screen with the text: "Enter your Zip Code." This seemed harmless enough, so I did, and then hit ENTER. The text was replaced by another message. "A representative will be contacting you shortly."

At this point, my entire computer shut off. I don't mean crashed – it simply switched itself off.

And before I could question what was going on, there was a knock at the door.

CHAPTER NINETEEN

SUMMONED

I should mention that it was just about midnight and Lally and Davin were fast asleep. At least, I hoped they were. A few times in the past, I've caught Lally texting her girlfriends in the middle of the night. (I hope they were girlfriends.) She very much wanted a webcam for her computer, but I doubted I'd let that happen until her 40th birthday.

Even if things had been normal, having someone knock on your door at midnight is an unsettling experience. The fact that this came right on the heels of me contacting a Devil worship group was downright frightening.

My mind raced with questions: Who's at the door? Was it The Brotherhood? How could they locate me with just a zip code? How could they have possibly arrived here so quickly? Who polished off the Nutella in the cabinet above the microwave? (When the mind races, it often goes off on tangents.)

There was only one way to get answers, and that was to open the door. I slowly made my way to the front door and asked, "Who is it? Who's there?"

"Is that you, Mr. Bolton?" came a voice from outside.

"Yes. Who are you?"

"I'm with the Brotherhood, Mr. Bolton. Would you kindly open the door so we can speak?"

What could I do? I'd gone this far, and I suppose there was no turning back. I swung the door open and....

I don't know what I was expecting. But had I been given a thousand guesses – a million guesses – I doubt I would have landed on who was at my door.

He was wearing blue-and-yellow shorts with a matching baseball cap. His toothy grin, which I'd seen so many time before, lit up my doorway like a lantern. Standing on my "Home Sweet Home" doormat was none other than Chuck E Cheese.

The situation was so surreal I actually lost my balance and stumbled back a few steps.

"Whoa, there!" said the huge mouse, catching me in his big, rubber hands. I realized that it wasn't really Chuck E. Cheese, but someone in a mouse costume. .

"Are you okay, mister?" asked the person in the suit.

"Uh, yeah. Who are you?"

"My name's not important."

"Is your grandma named Rita?" I asked. I actually didn't know if I was trying to be funny or not.

"No. She's dead. They both are."

"Oh, sorry," I said. "Well, what can I do for you?"

"I've been instructed to drive you somewhere," said the voice in the rubber head. He sounded like a teenager.

"Where?"

"To see The Dark Priest," he said. He tried to remove his hat, but it was apparently glued to Chuck E's head.

"The Dark Priest?" Where had I heard that name before? Ah! In the principal's office. Detective Zanderhoff had asked me if I knew The Dark Priest.

Before I could ask any questions, the mouse said, "C'mon, he's waiting. And you do not want to keep The Dark Priest waiting." He gestured toward a black sedan waiting at the end of my walk.

"Wait!" I said. "I have to take care of my kids first."

Chuck E. threw up his furry hands in frustration. He reached into his pocket and withdrew a pawful of prize tickets. "Here," he said, thrusting them into my hands. "This will keep them happy for awhile."

I took the tickets and went upstairs and gently tapped on Lally's door. I could hear a flurry of movement, but when I opened the door a crack, Lally was fast asleep. Ha, ha. "You can forget about the webcam," I announced.

"Wha?…" Lally yawned, pantomiming sleepiness like a silent-movie star. "Oh, Daddy? Is it time to go to school already?"

"No, Lillian Gish," I said, without even a ray of hope

she'd appreciate my sarcastic reference. "I have to run out and need you to keep an eye on Davin."

"Where're you going?"

It was amazingly satisfying to give her the answer she'd given me since she turned 12, "Out," I told her. "Just keep an eye on everything, okay? I'm trusting you."

"Okay," she said in a tone that I actually believed. As I turned to leave, she asked, "Dad, is everything okay?"

What could I tell her? "Don't worry, Daddy is just going with Chuck E. Cheese to meet The Dark Priest at a congregation of Devil worshippers so he can go to Hell and talk with Satan?" The most honest answer I could give was, "I hope so."

"If anything happens to you…" she began.

"I'll be fine."

"But if anything does…" she seemed to consider a few different options. "…Where'd you hide my pot?"

I smiled, threw a stuffed Spongebob at her, and then went downstairs to join Chuck E.

CHAPTER TWENTY
ALL HAIL THE DARK PRIEST

I found Chuck E. in the kitchen looking through my refrigerator. An image ran through my mind of Chuck E. Cheese stuck to a really gigantic glue trap.

"You ready?" he asked me, sniffing a bowl of pudding.

"Yeah, I…" then I thought of something. I took the Banjo From Hell out of the closet. "Okay, I'm all set," I told the gigantic mouse.

We left the house and walked toward the waiting sedan. "Can you really drive a car like that?" I asked.

"No. I don't even have a driver's license yet. I keep messing up the parallel parking," he confessed as we arrived at the car. He opened the rear door for me to get in.

I shouldn't have been surprised, but I was. The driver was someone else dressed in a Chuck E. Cheese costume.

"Headquarters," said Chuck E. Cheese number one. And the sedan sped off.

"Where are we going?" I asked stupidly.

"We can't tell you that," said Chuck. "In fact, I'm afraid we have to do…. this." From somewhere, he produced yet another rubber Chuck E. Cheese head and placed it over my own head. He put it on backwards so I couldn't see a thing.

The driver must have switched on the radio, because Lady Gaga's *I Like It Rough* blared from the speakers.

> *I'm shiny and I know it*
> *Don't know why you wanna blow it*
> *Need a man who likes it rough*
> *Likes it rough, likes it rough*

"You're a lucky guy," yelled Chuck E. over Lady Gaga.

"Why?"

"The Dark Priest doesn't grant audiences very often. It's quite an honor."

"Who is The Dark Priest?" I asked.

Driver Chuck E. Cheese laughed. "If he told you, he'd have to kill you. Then I'd have to kill him."

I couldn't tell if he was kidding or not. I decided to play it safe and not ask either mouse any more questions. We drove in silence for a little while. Every now and then the car would make a turn – I sensed that some of those turns were just to confuse me, which really wasn't necessary. Then the sedan slowed down and seemed to be traveling down a slope. The car stopped, and I heard something opening which I supposed was a garage door. Then the car moved forward, stopped, and I could hear the garage door lowering again.

"You can take off the mask now," I was told.

I took off the Chuck E. Cheese head to discover I was indeed in a huge garage of some sort. Driver Chuck E. helped me out of the back seat and both mice escorted me and my banjo down a long, cement corridor. At the end was a gray metal door.

"Good luck," said both mice in unison, then they turned and left.

To say I was nervous would be an understatement. I hadn't a clue what I'd find on the other side of that metal door. Oh, I'd seen plenty of corny horror movies where dark-robed figures in a candlelit chamber sat around a long table while the leader dressed in crimson robes conducted secret rituals. But this was reality, and I had no idea what to expect.

I took a deep breath and stepped through the door into a candlelit chamber. Dark robed figures sat around a long table. Their leader, dressed in crimson robes, held a huge, ornate goblet aloft. It blocked his face.

"*Abraxas voso astaroth*," he chanted.

""*Abraxas voso astaroth*," repeated the others..

"Welcome to the Brotherhood of Lucifer," said the leader, the goblet still blocking his face. "I am The Dark Priest."

"Hail The Dark Priest!" chanted the people around the table.

"Hi. Hail. Whatever," I said, unsure how to address him.

Nothing could have prepared me for the intense shock I received when The Dark Priest lowered the goblet. It was Walter.

CHAPTER TWENTY-ONE

THE TOAST

"**C**ome on in, Richard," said Walter the Dark Priest.

Dazed, I shuffled into the chamber. "Walter? You're The Dark Priest?"

"Yeah. Can we get you something? Fresca maybe?" asked The Dark Priest.

"What the hell are you doing here, Walter?!" I asked.

He grimaced. "Could you not call me that? Please?" he asked. "I'm The Dark Priest. Or D.P. will do."

"You're an actuary. You deal with insurance," I protested.

He shrugged. "Actuary by day. Conduit to the Prince of Darkness, Lord of the Underworld by night."

"Hail Lucifer!" chanted the robed men.

"Hail Lucifer," responded Walter automatically. "I'd do this full time, but it doesn't pay anything. I do get a monthly stipend for dry-cleaning the robes," he added.

"But you're…" 'How could I tell Walter he was too boring to be a Satanic high priest? "You're too boring to be a Satanic high priest!"

"Oh, please. Christian priests are boring. Rabbis are boring. Monks are boring. So where does it say that Satanic priests have to be Conan O'Brien?"

D.P. had a point.

"Besides, it gets me out of the house and away from Arlene. She's got her canasta, and I have this," he said, gesturing to the chamber and the robed supplicants.

"That's insane. She plays cards while you worship the Devil?" I said.

"Hey, *my* marriage is still intact, kiddo," he pointed out. I'll admit, it stung. "And I don't just worship the Devil. I'm the big cheese around here." To make his point, he held up his hand displaying a gaudy signet ring.

"All hail The Dark Priest," chanted the supplicants.

"See?" said Walter smugly.

"Who are these people?" I asked.

"People like us, who wish to harness the forces of evil and embrace the darkness that permeates everything and want to get out of the house for awhile," explained Walter.

"No, not people like *us*, Walter. People like *you*. I'm not part of this," I said.

Walter looked puzzled. "They why are you here?"

"Because of this," I said and held up the banjo.

The room erupted. Acolytes dashed around the chamber wailing and waving their hands like lunatics. Even Walter was stunned, standing motionless as the pandemonium unfolded. The candles flickered and the rumbling of thunder filled the air.

Eventually, Walter came to his senses and pounded a pewter goblet on the table. "Order! Brothers, bring yourself to order! Order!"

Eventually everyone calmed down and returned to their seats.

"Why is everyone carrying on?" I asked.

"A few years ago, I was just a member of this congregation like all the others," Walter explained. "But then I received…. The Toast."

"The Toast!" repeated the acolytes.

Walter assumed a commanding voice and bellowed, "Brothers, fetch The Toast!"

Two robed figures dashed off and returned with a gilded box. They presented it to Walter, bowing as they backed away and returned to their chairs.

"It was a morning like any other. Coffee – orange juice – and then THIS!" He opened the lid of the box to reveal an old piece of toast sitting on a satin pillow. The Toast had distinctive burn marks that looked vaguely similar to the markings on my banjo, though without the circles.

"It was unmistakable – the Toast bore the markings of Lucifer himself. An emergency meeting of the Brotherhood was convened and on that very night, I was named The Dark Priest."

"Makes sense to me," I said, eyeing the door and hoping it was still unlocked.

"But now, Richard, you've received a sign far greater than mine. Lucifer has spoken. Our course is clear..." And before I could realize what Walter was doing, he removed his crimson headpiece and placed it on my head.

"All hail The Dark Priest," he commanded.

"Hail The Dark Priest," they chanted as they bowed toward me.

CHAPTER TWENTY-TWO⊕
GIVE OR TAKE A PACKET OF SPLENDA

"Hey, stop that!" I said, removing the official Dark Priest hat. "I don't want to be your Dark Priest." And with that, I placed the goofy headpiece back on Walter's head.

"But…. But you received the sign," stammered Walter. "You've been chosen. You received the call!"

"I haven't received anything. It wasn't a call," I insisted. And then I told the entire story of Davin, and the Banjo/pawn ticket. When I was finished, a reverent hush filled the chamber.

"I see," said Walter. "You weren't chosen after all."

"Of course not," I said.

"Davin was!" he proclaimed. "Send the mice to fetch the boy!"

"No!" I screamed. "Absolutely not. We weren't called. But something is really wrong with my son – your wife's son. And I have to find out what it is. That's why I'm here. I need your help."

"What do you want us to do?" Walter asked, returning to his calm (dull) self.

"I need to.... " I paused. I just couldn't believe what I was about to say. "I need to ask Lucifer what he requires to get Mr. Peety back to us. I need to talk with Lucifer."

This last statement caused some serious murmuring among the Devil worshippers. As the members chattered, I could detect one word popping up through the din… Elixir.

Walter appeared lost in thought and then seemed to reach a decision. "Richard, there might be a way. But there are risks."

"I'm desperate," I admitted. "It's for my boy."

"Very well," he said. "Bring the Elixir!"

The robed figures chanted "Elixir. Elixir. Elixir," and one member disappeared down a dark passage.

"When I joined the Brotherhood," said Walter, "the Elixir was already here. Some say it's *always* been here. Nobody knows where it came from or even what it does for certain. But its power is said to be very great indeed."

The man returned with a bottle of Zima.

"Zima?" I asked. "That's the Elixir?"

"No," said Walter. "We put it in a Zima bottle to make sure nobody drinks it."

They had me climb onto the table with the banjo and sit in the absolute center facing south. As the acolytes chanted something in an ancient and forgotten tongue, I was instructed to drink the Elixir.

I brought the bottle to my lips, then hesitated. "You sure it's not Zima?"

"Positive," said Walter.

I downed half the contents in one gulp. The taste is a bit hard to describe, but I'll try. Imagine a bottle of cheap gin that has been passed around between seven winos. Now imagine that bottle was tossed away and the mixture of backwash and gin at the bottom is left to fester in a dark alley for a month or two. Now imagine a glass with an old woman's dentures soaking in it. Take that stuff in the gin bottle and pour it into the denture glass, remove the teeth, and add sixteen packets of Splenda. Now imagine drinking that. That's sort of what it tasted like, give or take a Splenda packet.

For a brief moment I wanted to hurl, but then everything went totally black and totally silent. I suppose that I passed out, and it's even possible that I died. I no longer had the urge to throw up. I no longer had the urge for *anything*. I could not even tell if my eyes were open or not. I think they were, but then I heard a thunderous slamming sound. Then I heard it again. It took me a moment to realize it was the sound of my own eyelids blinking. The sound was deafening, and I decided to keep my eyes shut. Now the only thing I could hear was a repetitive thumping that shook the floor – I knew instinctively it was the sound of my heart beating.

And then I felt the heat.

CHAPTER TWENTY-THREE
THE PORTAL OF GUGALANNA

People are always quick to use the expression "Hot as Hell." When you bought this book, you were probably hoping for some never-before-revealed insights into Hell. Well, I'll try not to disappoint you more than I already have. So, here's the first thing you probably don't know...

Hell is not all that hot. Oh, it's hot, alright. Vegas in August is a Kenmore refrigerator compared to the heat of Hell. But it's not the searing, eternal fire that burns the skin to a crisp so that your flesh falls from your bones in molten globs. It's not that hot, but in a way it's more evil.

The thing about the heat of Hell is that there's always a slight hint that things might improve. Every so often, there's a delicate little breeze – a suggestion of coolness that fills your heart with hope that the heat will soon pass. So it's not the searing heat that tortures you, but the occasional little cool breeze.

So I felt the heat as I lay with my cheek pressed against a hard, smooth surface. Since my eyes were shut, I assumed I was still up on the table.

"Wake up, Mr. Bolton," said a strange, squeaky voice.

"Walter?" I said, afraid or unable to open my eyes.

"Uh, uh," said the squeaky voice. "Guess again?"

"Chuck E. Cheese?"

"No," said the squeaky voice, a little disappointed. " I'll give you a hint."

The voice made a series of sounds. *"Teedle-dee-dee-dee-dee dee-dee-dee. Teedle-dee-dee-dee-dee dee-dee-dee."*

At first I had no idea what it was. And then I recognized the melody – It was Dueling Banjos.

I squeezed my eyes even tighter shut and said, "Carl?"

"Bingo!" said the squeaky voice. "Come on, open up. I don't bite. Actually, I do. Quite hard. But I won't bite you unless you make me mad."

"What makes you mad?" I dared to ask.

"People who don't open their eyes when I ask them to. That's something that really pisses me off."

I opened my eyes. I was lying on polished stone, and directly in front of me were a pair of monstrously huge eyes. When I was a kid, there was a local optometrist who had a jumbo pair of glasses hanging outside his store. These glasses would have fit Carl just about right.

"Let me be the first to welcome you to Hell, Richard," said Carl the Boogeyman.

Carl scrambled to his feet and then grabbed me by the

armpits and helped me up. Carl the Boogeyman was a giant – small as giants go, I suppose, but a giant nevertheless. Everything about him was massive, especially his hands. He caught me looking at them.

"Yeah, I know they're big. That whole banjo thing was a bad idea, huh?" he said, pointing at the Gibson Florentine Vox-4.

"Maybe you should try the drums," I suggested.

His face lit up as if this had never occurred to him. "The drums!" he said, testing how it sounded. "Yes, I can play the drums!"

I didn't think for a moment that I was dreaming. As absurd and impossible as the situation was, I knew without an inkling of doubt that this was really, truly happening. Just as you know you are reading a book right now (or an e-book, if you went that route), I knew I was in the dark realm of Lucifer. A sign that read "Welcome to the Dark Realm of Lucifer" only added to my conviction.

"It's hot," I said.

"Sorry, the AC's on the fritz. Been broken since Day One," he said. He laughed and then slapped me on the back for good measure. He might have dislodged a few vertebrae.

Looking around, I noticed I was standing on a cliff atop an insanely high precipice. A sheer wall of rock plunged straight down, disappearing into a brownish smog. The only way off the cliff was through a portal carved directly into the rock. "That must be the Portal of Gugalanna," I observed, amazed that I'd remembered the name.

"That it is," he said with a glint of admiration in his eyes. Then, quite serious, "But to get inside, you'll need The Key of Wallawegnon. You brought it with you, right?"

My stomach lurched with a sudden wave of despair. "The Key of *what*?"

He stared at me intently, and then broke into a huge laugh. "Ahh, I'm just messin' with ya'!" His smile revealed a few sets of jagged, razor-sharp teeth. "Come on," he said cheerfully, "The Boss wants to see you."

And with that, Carl the Boogeyman turned and walked through the Portal of Gugalanna. I clutched the banjo tightly and began to follow. I paused briefly at the Portal, took a deep breath, and then walked into Hell.

CHAPTER TWENTY-FOUR

THE PITS

The first thing I noticed was the disco music. I believe it was Cheryl Lynn's *Got To Be Real*. I absolutely loathe disco music, and I couldn't believe I was hearing it now.

What you find-a
(I think I love you baby)
What you feel now
(I feel I need you baby)
What you know-a
To be real!

"What's with the music?" I asked Carl, trying not to sound too annoyed.

"Hah," he responded. "What are you hearing?"

I couldn't understand why he was asking me that. "Some old disco thing," I answered.

"Don't like disco music, huh?" he responded.

"No. Hate it in fact."

"That's why you're hearing it, " he explained. "Everyone

down here has their own personal soundtrack of the music they hate the most. Currently, I believe Britney Spears' *Till The World Ends* is playing in the most people's heads. Barney's *I Love You, You Love Me* often tops the list. For a brief time in the 80's, a Kellogg's Raisin Bran jingle was driving everyone nuts. People were running into walls shouting 'Two scoops! Two scoops!' It was pretty frightening."

"Can't you turn it off?" I pleaded.

"Maybe the Boss can. You can ask him when you meet him," he said. "Hey, you're lucky you're just a visitor – for now."

I didn't like the sound of that "for now." To make things worse, Donna Summer's *MacArthur Park* had just begun…

I don't think that I can take it
'cause it took so long to bake it
And I'll never have that recipe again

But, I decided to drop the subject and tried to tune it out.

I had expected a cavern or a tunnel carved through rough rock, so I was surprised to see we were walking down an ordinary hallway. Too ordinary, in fact. There were beige sheetrock walls with an occasional Norman Rockwell or Leroy Neiman print. Fluorescent light fixtures were set into a white suspended ceiling. The hall could just as easily have been in a corporate office or municipal building, except for two things. The hall seemed to go on forever and there were hundreds, perhaps thousands, of doors on either side.

"What's behind these doors?" I asked Carl the Boogeyman.

"Pits. Lots of pits."

"Pits?"

"Yeah. Take a look if you want. The Boss said I could show you around," he said congenially.

I paused before a gray door. A side of me said, "Are you crazy? Don't look at anything. Just take care of business and get out of here." But another side of me said, "This is a once in a lifetime experience. You have to look."

Carl said, "Who are you talking to?"

I hadn't realized my "sides" we actually speaking out loud. Five minutes in Hell and I was already losing it. I turned the doorknob and swung open the door.

The room was roughly a 20-foot square. The walls were decorated with posters of nude women and magazine centerfold, and in the center of the room was a circular pit. From where I was standing, I could not see the bottom. I heard a scrambling noise that sounded sort of like paper rustling. Soon, a balding man's head appeared just over the lip of the pit. As soon as his eyes cleared the rim, something miraculous happened – the nude posters on the wall were suddenly all clothed!

The man popped his head over the top and quickly looked around the room. "Shit!" he said. "Shit! Shit! Shit!" Then he saw me, "Hey!" he said.

"Hey," I replied.

"What were they wearing?" he asked.

"Who?"

"The chicks in the posters."

"Nothing. Not a thing."

"Shit!" he repeated. "I knew it! Fuck!" And with that, he tumbled back down into the pit. The posters immediately reverted to their nude, erotic states.

I walked up to the rim of the pit and peered down. The man was sprawled over a bunch of porno magazines. Apparently he had stacked them to climb up the side of the pit and look out. I gathered that there were just enough magazines for him to look over the top, but not enough to actually escape.

"Please. Describe the posters to me," he begged.

"Nude women. Big breasts. That sort of thing," I offered. I really wasn't comfortable going into too much detail. "Why don't you just look at your magazines?" I suggested.

"Oh, thank you. I've only been here like twenty-three years, I should have thought of that," he blurted sarcastically. "Look!"

He picked up a copy of Vixen Sluts and held up the centerfold to me. A truly trashy redhead posed on a bale of hay, legs spread. She was sexy as can be, except that she was wearing a denim shirt and overalls that might have been borrowed from a Nebraskan pig farmer.

He showed me a succession of sexy women, all totally clothed. I got the point.

"I can't stand it!" he screamed. "Not a tit. Not a butt crack. Nothing!"

"Must be rough."

"Brilliant deduction," he said, being sarcastic yet again. I decided I didn't like this fellow very much.

"The Beatles music doesn't help any, either," he added.

Yeah. I didn't like this guy at *all*. I turned and began to leave.

"Wait," cried the man in the pit. "Does Dolly Parton still have huge jugs?"

I returned to the hall, closing the door behind me.

CHAPTER TWENTY-FIVE

VONNEGUT NO, HEMINGWAY YES

S o that was the Pit of Hell. Well, one of them, anyway. I checked out a few more as we progressed down the endless fluorescent-lit hallway.

One pit had a woman with a bunch of jigsaw puzzles, and each puzzle was missing one piece. Invariably, it was a crucial piece, such as the Pinocchio's nose or the torch on the Statue of Liberty.

Another pit contained a very fat man and a huge buffet laid out for him. A sign on the wall read "All You Can Eat." At first this seemed like an idea situation, except as soon as the guy had one bite, he completely lost his appetite.

A fellow in a top hat and tweed suit was kept company by an old-fashioned stock ticker. He would read the ticker tape as it was dispensed and howl in agony. He was able to witness the vast sums his investments were yielding with no way to access them.

As I left, Carl said, "That's one of my favorites. We got the idea from Kurt Vonnegut."

"He's down here?" I asked, shocked.

"I wish," said Carl, wistfully. "It was in one of his books."

In a way, this revelation shocked me more than anything I'd seen so far. The Boogeyman was a fan of Kurt Vonnegut novels. "Hemingway's down here, though," he said.

"Ernest Hemingway didn't go to Heaven?" I asked incredulously.

"Oh, he did," said Carl. "But he put in a request to come down here. He's an interesting guy, but once he starts drinking you can't shut him up."

CHAPTER TWENTY-SIX
THE EXPLANATION

After walking for miles, the end of the hallway finally came into view. Though it was far away, I could tell the passageway was blocked by a door of some kind.

"This is an awful lot of walking," I said. "Why don't you get a golf cart or something?"

"I requisitioned one of those Segue scooter things," he answered, "but Lucifer nixed the idea. He said we have an image to maintain, and those things look simply ridiculous."

By this point, I had lost all sense of direction, though I got the feeling we were gradually heading down. Also, I had totally lost track of time. There were no clocks and my wristwatch somehow read 6:66.

"So, whaddya wanna see next?" asked the Boogeyman, congenially. "The Fire of Damnation? Chamber of Eternal Despair? The Cafeteria?"

"You have a cafeteria?" I asked incredulously.

"Oh, yes. Adolf Eichmann makes a killer Mac 'N' Cheese."

I decided to pass. I had a mission to accomplish and, as much as it scared me, I thought it time to get down to business. "I think I should meet…." I simply could not bring myself to finish the sentence. "You know, get it over with."

"I hear you," said Carl, nodding. "Time to take the bull by the horns, so to speak," he chortled.

We continued on to the door at the end of the corridor. It was a lot further away than I had thought. By the time we arrived, I realized the door was enormous. The door was made of rough-hewn iron with a human skull imbedded in the center.

"State your business," said the skull, much to my amazement.

"Hey, Jeffrey. We're here to see the Boss," said the Boogeyman.

"Oh, we are, are we?" said the skull in a haughty tone. "He happens to be in a very bad mood."

"That book again?" asked Carl

"What else," answered the skull. If he had had shoulders he would have shrugged. "Anyhow, he's not entertaining visitors."

Carl turned to me and said, "Show Jeff the banjo."

I pushed in front of Carl and held up the banjo for the skull to read the runes.

His draw dropped in a way that was both comical and

creepy at the same time. "Wow," he said. "Wow. Wow," he said again. There were metallic sounds of bolts sliding and tumblers turning, and the massive door swung open with a loud creak.

"Have fun, champ," said the skull. "But don't say I didn't warn you."

As we entered, Carl said, "Ah, pay no mind to him. Dahmer's a pain in the ass to everyone."

I cast a glance back toward the door. The skull said "Wow!" one more time as the door slammed shut.

Now things looked a bit more like I'd expected Hell to appear. I'd entered something that resembled a gothic church, but built on a unimaginably huge scale. The pointed arches disappeared into the shadows high overhead. Stained glass windows lined the walls depicting scenes of hideous cruelty and torture. In one, hooded clerics poured molten lead into a woman's ear. In another, a huge masked man in a loincloth flayed another man with a spiked whip. In a third window, men in business suits waterboarded a guy in a turban.

Every few paces, a hideous gargoyle protruded from the wall. To my horror, I noticed that they were not stone, but actual living creatures of some sort. I was even more surprised when they spoke to me. "Hey, Tex, is that a banjo in your hand or are you just glad to see me?" said one. As we walked down the nave, a few of the gargoyles chanted, "Lions and tigers and bears! Oh my! Lions and tigers and bears! Oh my!" They thought it was funny, but I had a sudden urge to turn and run out of the cathedral. I reminded myself I was doing this for Davin, steeled my courage, and pushed on.

At the end of the aisle, a huge desk rested in the middle of the cathedral's transept. Behind it sat a small, harried man in a shirt and tie. He was talking on the telephone and held up a finger to us and mouthed "one sec," then continued his conversation.

"What? The book's in Asia, too? Well, that really sucks." He scribbled something down on a pad. I didn't know who he was speaking with, but the poor fellow was getting more upset by the second. "Hey, *I* know it's bullshit. And *you* know it's bullshit. But readers are eating that crap up!"

I incorrectly assumed that he was like the other people I saw in the pits, doomed to live out eternal frustration.

"Yes, I know it's not gonna go away all on its own. I'll think of something. Just keep me updated, will you? Caio," he said, then hung up the phone. "Can you believe those assholes?" he asked me, as if I knew what he was talking about. Then he noticed the banjo. "Ahhhhhh! You must be Richard!" he said.

"Uh, yeah," I replied.

Carl noticed my confusion. "Mr. Bolton, permit me to introduce you to Lucifer, Prince of Lost Souls, Lord of Darkness, Ruler of…"

"Yes, yes," said Lucifer, impatiently. He rose from his chair and offered his hand. "Welcome, Richard. Welcome, indeed."

I shook Lucifer's hand. For the briefest moment, my mind filled with the worst memories of my life. Hitting my head on a diving board. Witnessing my Grandpa Clarence falling down a flight of stairs. Taking my kids to see *Star*

Wars: Revenge of the Sith.

"Sorry about that," he said, withdrawing his hand. "Be happy you didn't kiss me," he said with a laugh.

The man in front of me looked totally ordinary – maybe five-ten, slightly balding, a bit paunchy, even.

"You're really the Devil?" I asked.

"Not what you expected, eh?" he said with a laugh. "This is kinda like Match.com – the dates never quite look like their photos. Sorry to disappoint you."

"Uh, I'm not disa…" .

"Jesus got all the good genes. Tall. Thin. Great hair. I was an afterthought," he said, bitterly. "We don't actually have genes, of course, but you get the idea."

"Sure," I lied.

He stepped from behind his desk and showed me his pointed tail and cloven feet. "There. Is that more what you had in mind?"

I think I nodded.

"Ahhh – I see you brought the pawn ticket!" said Lucifer, pointing at the Gibson Florentine Vox-4. He opened a drawer in his desk and pulled out a little torture rack. Mr. Peety the giraffe was stretched out on it. "Let's do business."

I gulped and spoke the line I had rehearsed over and over, "I need Mr. Peety back and I want you to leave my little boy alone."

"Of course you do, Richard. And nothing would make me happier. But Davin owes me something. And unless I get it, Mr. Peety stays on the rack," he said, turning the handle on the miniature torture device and stretching the giraffe's neck even longer. "And little Davin will... well, let's just say he's not going to fit in at school very well." He twisted the little wheel a bit more.

"Will you stop that!" I shouted.

"Uh, oh," said Carl the Boogeyman.

A deathly silence filled the cathedral. This was followed by the sound of gargoyles scurrying up to safety. From the other side of the cathedral I could just make out Jeffrey Dahmer saying, "You are *sooo* fucked."

Lucifer's eyes briefly burned with dark fire, but then he smiled. "Everyone just relax, okay? Mr. Bolton is new here, so I'll cut him a little slack." The gargoyles scurried back to their positions.

"I'm sorry," I said. "But I don't know what you want. What could I possibly owe you, Satan?"

This time the gargoyles took flight and smashed right through the stained glass windows. Jeffrey Dahmer said, "Fucked. Fucked. And double fucked!" Carl buried his face in his huge hands.

Lucifer's eyes flared again, and this time the entire cathedral shook. Chunks of plaster and shards of glass showered down around us. The Devil stared at me and I was certain I would be reduced to ashes on the spot. "You give me no choice, Mr. Bolton," he said, turning his attention to the little rack. He began turning and turning the wheel, stretching Mr. Peety's neck to near decapitation.

"No!" I screamed. "I beg you. Please. It won't happen again!"

"Are you sure?" asked Lucifer, giving the wheel another turn. I could see the seams spreading on the stuffed toy.

"Yes, I swear to G…" I caught myself. "I promise."

"Very well," he said, and loosened the rack a few notches.

"But I don't understand. What does Davin owe you?"

"One soul, Mr. Bolton. Simple as that. A soul," explained Lucifer.

"I don't get it. How could my boy possibly owe you a soul?" I asked.

Lucifer sighed and opened another drawer in his desk. He took out a manila folder, opened it, and then removed an 8x10 photograph. "Do you recognize this man, Richard?" he asked, handing me the picture.

I took the photo and recognized the man immediately – it was the mug shot of the serial murderer who was in the hospital the same time as Davin. "It's Raymond Pizutto," I said. "What's he got to do with anything?"

"Mr. Pizutto has *everything* to do with our current problem, Richard," said Lucifer. "You see, he was supposed to have died in the hospital. We had something very, very special waiting for him, too." For a moment, Lucifer's thoughts seemed to drift off, imagining that special something.

"But he didn't die," I said, unnecessarily.

"Exactly. That three-ring circus you call a health care system bent over backwards to save his sorry ass. It's amazing what your doctor's can concoct if you throw enough money at them," he said angrily. "So when my Harvester of Souls arrived to claim him, he was eating Cozy Shack Rice Pudding and watching Family Feud."

I shuddered, realizing where this was going.

"Meanwhile, your sweet little boy was getting worse and worse because you had a worthless health plan. The Soul Harvester is loyal, but not too bright. He knew he had to get someone, and your kid seemed like the only ready candidate, so he snatched him up."

Suddenly, all the insanity of the recent weeks made a lot more sense.

"Nobody knew what to do with Davin," the Devil continued. "It was clear he didn't belong down here, but I couldn't just let him go, either. After all, I was out a prized soul. It would set a bad precedent. Finally, I let him go back, but a little..." He smiled wickedly. "A little *changed*. And holding Mr. Peety here until I got what I deserved," he concluded.

"And you gave him my banjo," said Carl, dejectedly.

"That plinking of yours was driving me up the freakin' walls, Carl," said the Devil.

"I was gettin' better," countered Carl.

"Better? Yeah, right. It sounded like…"

"Hey, can we focus here? " I interrupted. "I understand what happened. But what am I supposed to do?"

"Well, Richard," said Lucifer, draping his arm around my shoulder like we were old school buddies. "You owe me a soul, so you're gonna have to get me a soul."

"Whose soul?" I asked, fearing the answer.

"Raymond Pizutto's, Richard," answered Lucifer, the picture of patience and understanding. "Get Pizutto's evil butt down here and you and your boy are free-and-clear."

"But…" I said.

Before I could finish, the world changed.

CHAPTER TWENTY-SEVEN

A VERY NICE COFFEE SHOP

"Is he dead?" I heard someone ask.

"No," said someone else. "Look, he's waking up!"

I opened my eyes expecting to see Carl the Boogeyman, but instead I was looking at Walter.

"You okay, Richard?" he asked.

"Uh, yeah," I managed to say.

"I don't know what happened. That stuff was supposed to work," he said apologetically, pointing to the half-empty Zima bottle.

"It did work, Walter," I said.

"Call me Dark Priest, will you?" he whispered. "And what do you mean it worked? You just sipped it a few seconds ago."

I was about to tell them everything I experienced, but then reconsidered. If I had to get Raymond Pizutto's soul down to Hell, it might involve doing things that no one should know about. "I mean, it worked at giving me a really bad headache. Thanks a lot, Walter!" I said while rubbing my forehead.

"Dark Priest, Richard. Dark Priest!" he hissed.

While they were helping me off the table, I slipped the Elixir into my coat pocket, just on the chance I would need it again.

"Thanks for wasting my time," I said. "Which way's the door?"

One of the acolytes pointed to the exit.

"Hey, Richie, don't mention any of this to Arlene, okay?" said The Dark Priest. "She thinks I'm at a conference in Phoenix."

With the banjo firmly in my grip, I marched out the door and into the night air.

There was one problem – I had no idea where I was. The two Chuck E. Cheese's had my head covered with a mask while they drove me to the secret location. With no other choice, I picked a random direction and began walking.

I had only progressed fifty yards or so when I heard a voice. "Out for a late night stroll, Mr. Bolton?"

I froze. That voice – I recognized it from somewhere. It took me a moment, but then it hit me. I turned to notice a parked sedan with the passenger side window rolled down.

"Detective Zanderhoff," I said, feeling somewhat weak in the knees.

"Yep. You seem a bit lost. Hop in, we'll give you a ride home."

I took a deep, sad breath and climbed into the back seat.

"You remember Officer Gallagher," said Zanderhoff.

Gallagher snorted. "*No. I never heard of the Dark Priest,*" he said, in a mocking voice, which I suppose was meant to sound like me.

"So how long have you been attending these little Satanic jamborees?" asked the detective.

"This was my first time," I said.

"In a pig's eye," said Gallagher.

"Really. Two..." I was going to tell them that two Chuck E. Cheese's came to get me, but decided that would make me sound like a complete lunatic. "Two people came to my door and told me the Dark Priest wanted to see me."

"Uh, huh," said Zanderhoff, not believing a word I said. He looked me in the eye and said, "Mr. Bolton, I've been a cop for a long time."

"A *very* long time," echoed Officer Gallagher.

"And I've met more than my share of lunatics and bad eggs," he continued.

"*Way* more than his share," said Gallagher.

"You don't strike me as either, Mr. Bolton. But I'm gettin' the feeling you're in over your head in something," said Zanderhoff.

"*Way* over your head," emphasized Gallagher.

"You know that's annoying," said Zanderhoff.

"*Very* annoying," stressed Gallagher, not realizing the conversation had shifted to him.

Detective Zanderhoff sighed and continued, "It's clear you're in trouble, Richard. So why don't you just tell us what's going on?"

We both waited for Gallagher to say something useless, but this time he didn't.

It was the middle of the night in the middle of nowhere. I was tired, worn-out, and frustrated. And I made one of the most important decisions of my life.

"Is there a place around here where we can talk?" I asked.

Zanderhoff smiled for the first time since I met him. "I know a nice coffee shop," he said.

"A *very* nice coffee shop," said Gallagher.

CHAPTER TWENTY-EIGHT

LUCKY MAN

As we sat in a corner booth at the Plainview Diner, I told Detective Zanderhoff everything. At his request, I didn't leave out any details. I told him about the Hula Harry's Chocolate Macadamia Coconut Clusters and the trip to the hospital. I talked about Mr. Peety, Raymond Pizutto, and the strange blocks in Mrs. Huvey's kindergarten class. Through all this he sat impassively, taking notes now and then. But when I got to Carl the Boogeyman and the Banjo From Hell, he stopped scribbling and looked up from his pad.

"The Boogeyman's name is Carl?" he asked, without even the hint of a smile.

"Yes," I answered.

"And he plays the banjo?"

"He tried to. His fingers are too thick," I explained.

Zanderhoff took a sip of his coffee. "Go on," he said.

So I told him about the trip to St. Blaise's and Father Ryan's reaction to the Gibson Florentine Vox-4. About the only thing I left out was Lally's hidden marijuana stash.

He let me talk and talk, but when I got to the visit with Dr. Lapinksy and Rita Notimportant, he stopped me.

"Her name was Notimportant?" asked Detective Zanderhoff.

"Uh, huh. And it was Notimportant who solved the riddle of the banjo," I said.

Officer Gallagher laughed. "You guys sound like Abbott and Costello," he said with corn muffin crumbs tumbling out of his mouth.

Zanderhoff cast an angry glance at Gallagher, then turned back to me. "What happened next," he asked.

"You're not gonna believe the next part," I told him.

"You're assuming I believe what you already told me," he said deadpan.

So I told him of my Internet search for a way to get to Hell and how I ended up at the Brotherhood of Lucifer.

"Who's the Dark Priest?" he asked.

I paused. I thought it over a second, then said, "Fuck it. He's my Ex-wife's husband Walter."

"We knew that," said Gallagher. "The Detective was just testing you."

"You passed," said Zanderhoff. "What happened next?"

I closed my eyes for a moment and gathered my thoughts. I was certain they'd think I was lying or completely nuts.

"Just tell us, Richard," urged Zanderhoff.

So I dove in and told them about my entire journey to Hell – The Portal of Gugalanna, the Pits, the Dahmer Door, Lucifer – everything. "You may not believe me," I told both men. "But I know for a fact, Hell is for real!"

There was complete silence at our booth, which was eventually broken by the sound of Gallagher slurping up the last of his milkshake through a straw.

"So you owe Lucifer Raymond Pizutto's soul?" summarized Zanderhoff.

"If I want Davin to get back to normal, yes," I replied.

Gallagher turned to Zanderhoff and asked like a school kid, "Oooo! Let me tell him. Let me tell him."

"Tell me what?" I asked.

"Mr. Bolton, you are a very lucky man," said Detective Zanderhoff.

"Lucky? Lucifer is controlling my son, holding his favorite toy hostage, and making impossible demands. How on earth am I lucky?!" I asked.

"Raymond Pizutto is back in the hospital," said Zanderhoff. "The asshole got into another knife fight. This time he's not expected to make it."

"Hey, I wanted to tell him!" whined Gallagher.

CHAPTER TWENTY-NINE

INFINITE MERCY

T he siren blared as Officer Gallagher sped toward the hospital while Detective Zanderhoff called ahead. I sat in the back, thankful for this amazing piece of good fortune.

Zanderhoff put away his phone and filled us in. "His condition is critical. 'Very grave' was the exact term the doctor used."

"Sweet!" said Gallagher.

"Kyle, is that siren really necessary?" asked Zanderhoff.

Officer Gallagher killed the siren. I finally got to ask a question that was on my mind since the diner. "Detective, you really believe my story?"

Zanderhoff turned back towards me and said, "In one word... yes. In my line of work, I've seen all sorts of things that just can't be explained. I'm a damn-good detective, and reaching conclusions is what I do best. And I long ago concluded that there's stuff going down that simply defies any logical explanation."

"I was abducted by UFO's once," offered Officer Gallagher.

"See? Stuff like that," said Zanderhoff. "There's no logical explanation why Gallagher here was ever hired to be a cop."

We arrived at the Mid-Long Island General Hospital and parked in a spot designated for "Doctors Only."

"Screw 'em," said Zanderhoff as we hopped out of the car.

The three of us raced in and were directed to the Intensive Care Unit.

The door to the ICU slid open and a very pretty, but very serious, nurse stopped us.

"We need to see Raymond Pizutto," said Zanderhoff, flashing his badge.

"Put that away," ordered the nurse. "Mr. Pizutto is in no shape for company."

"It's very important," I pleaded.

There must have been something in my voice, because she visibly softened. "Well, have a seat and wait. He's being attended to right now," she told us.

The three of us sat on some nearby chairs. Gallagher asked if he could hold the Banjo from Hell, and I handed it to him. He plucked a few notes before the nurse shushed him.

After about five minutes or so, Zanderhoff asked, "How long will the doctor be with him?"

"Oh, Mr. Pizutto isn't with a doctor," said the nurse. "To be honest, there's nothing the doctors can do for him at this point."

For some reason, a wave of fear shot through me. "Then who's he with?" I asked, more loudly than I had intended.

"Sssshhhh," said the nurse. "He's with a priest."

It took about three seconds for Zanderhoff and me to realize what that meant. "Oh, shit!" we said in unison. The two of us pushed passed the nurse and ran down the corridor to Pizutto's room. Clueless, Gallagher followed.

Raymond Pizutto was hooked up to every type of medical machine imaginable. At least a dozen drips hung on poles over his bed. Apparently, the county was making sure that this mass murderer died in the most expensive manner possible.

And beside all this kneeled Father Ryan. "Do you truly and humbly confess your sins?" he asked.

"Yes," said Pizutto, barely audible.

"What are you doing?" I demanded.

Father Ryan looked up, startled. At first he didn't recognize me, but then he saw the banjo. "You?! What are you doing here?"

"No, what are you doing here," I countered.

"This lost soul wishes to repent and be accepted back into the bosom of Christ," said the Priest.

"But he killed five people!" I said.

"And I'm really, really sorry," sputtered Pizutto.

"And four dogs!" added Gallagher.

"He's confessed it all," said Father Ryan. "Jesus has infinite mercy for the truly repentant."

"Like me," moaned Pizutto.

Father Ryan turned back to his Bible, "*Their sins and lawless acts I will remember no more, for they are like lost sheep returned to the flock. By the blood of Jesus, their guilt shall be cleansed and they shall be deemed fit to enter the Most Holy Place.*

Father Ryan reached into his bag and took out a vile of Holy Water.

"No! Stop that!" I yelled. Without even thinking, I ran over and tried to grab the Holy Water from him.

Father Ryan moved it out of my reach. "Raymond, do you accept Jesus as your Lord and Savior?" he asked.

"Yes, I do," said Pizutto.

"Give that to me," I said, wrestling with the surprisingly strong Priest.

"Do you humbly and sincerely seek forgiveness from the infinite love of Jesus?" asked the Priest as he kneed me in the balls.

"Yes," said Pizutto in a hoarse whisper.

"*Ordo ad faciendam awuam benedictam*," I heard Father Ryan say. I climbed to my feet to see the Priest sprinkling Holy Water on the dying murderer. "*Ego te absolvo a peccatis tuis*," he continued. "I absolve thee of thy sins."

"Bingo," said Raymond Pizutto. An angelic smile crossed his cracked lips, and then his eyes gently fluttered closed. The monitors around his bed flatlined and issued a steady tone.

Zanderhoff, Gallagher, and I stood there staring at the dead killer. "He's with Jesus now," said Father Ryan.

Over the flatline tone and the sounds of nurses and doctors racing toward our room, I could have sworn I heard Jeffrey Dahmer say, "You are *soooooo* fucked!"

CHAPTER THIRTY
NO OPTIONS

D
awn was just breaking as the sedan pulled up in front of my house. Though it had only been five or six hours, it seemed like I'd been to hell and back. And this was true, both figuratively and literally.

Zanderhoff handed me his card, "You call me before you do anything drastic, you hear me?" he said.

"I will," I lied, and stepped out of the car with the banjo. "And thanks for trying."

Zanderhoff tipped his hat and the car sped away.

When I entered the house, everything was as quiet and as I had left it. Not wanting to wake the kids, I tiptoed up the steps and peeked into Lally's room. She was fast asleep for real this time, snuggled up like a child with her Blackberry.

Then I peeked into Davin's room and the blood in my veins turned to ice.

Davin was fast asleep, too. But the walls of his room were completely covered with ancient runes and demonic symbols. I knew immediately that Davin had written them himself – they were in crayon and none of the writings were any higher than my 6-year-old could reach.

I quietly closed the door and went back downstairs. I walked into the kitchen and flipped on the light, half-expecting a zombie or something. But it all looked normal – for now. There was a message from Walter on the answering machine asking if I'd gotten home okay and saying I should be receiving a membership card in the mail.

I really didn't have any option. I sat down at the kitchen table and took the Zima bottle out of my coat pocket. I unscrewed the top and, clutching the banjo, drank what was left of the Elixir.

CHAPTER THIRTY-ONE
CALLING IN THE DEBT

My eyes were closed, but I knew I was back on the ledge. Like before, it was very hot and my cheek was pressed against polished rock that was only slightly cooler. My head was filled with a dreadful thumping sound which at first I attributed to the Elixir. But then other percussion sounds joined in, and when I heard a cymbal crash, I opened my eyes.

Just outside the Portal of Gugalanna sat Carl playing an elaborate drum set. Well, "playing" might be overgenerous – "brutalizing" might be more appropriate. When Carl saw my eyes were open, he put down the drumsticks and came over.

"Hey, Richard," said the Boogeyman.

"Hi, Carl. Nice drums."

"It was such a great idea, Richard. Thanks."

With no effort whatsoever, he lifted me up and helped dust off my clothing.

"Boy, I'm sure glad I'm not you today," he said.

"You know about it?" I asked.

"You kiddin' me? Something like this, we all know about," he explained.

"What's gonna happen?" I asked.

"No telling, kiddo. Some people think the Boss is slipping because of the book. And now this Pizutto thing?" Carl grimaced just thinking about it. "It makes the Boss look bad, Richard. *Real* bad."

I didn't know what book he was referring to. Lucifer had been complaining about a book when I first met him. I thought perhaps he meant the Bible.

"I know you just got a tough break, but the Boss might have to make an example of you," he said. "And the one thing you *don't* want to be down here is an example," he added with a look of pity in his eyes. When the Boogeyman pities you, you *know* you're in real trouble.

"Does he want to see me?" I asked.

"Does the Pope shit in the woods?" he responded, then turned and walked through the Portal of Gugalanna. I sighed the sigh of the damned, and followed.

"By the way," added Carl, "we actually have photographs."

"Of what?"

"The Pope. The Pope shitting in the woods. It was Pope Benedict XV in the Hürtgen Forest in 1921. Wanna see 'em?" he asked, trying to keep the mood light.

"Maybe later," I said, my mind on other things.

One of the "other things" was the disco music – The Village People were already singing *In The Navy. You better get used to it,* I warned myself.

I followed Carl a bit deeper into the passage, then we both stopped. Blocking our path were two, shiny-new Segue Scooters.

"Far out!" said Carl.

"He's really in a hurry to see me, huh?" I asked unnecessarily.

"Looks that way. Grab one and let's roll."

So we each hopped on a Segue and raced down the corridor of Hell. As we sped past countless doors to countless pits, I wondered which door I would soon be behind.

Way too quickly, we arrived at the Dahmer Door.

"Knock-a knock," said the skull in a playful, fake Italian accent.

I shook my head. The torment had already begun.

"Knock-a knock," he repeated.

"Who's there?" I replied.

"Theodore," said Jeffrey.

"Theodore who?"

"The a-door says you are a soooooooo fucked!" he said. As he laughed, the door swung open.

"That was really stupid," chastised Carl.

"Oh, I am *so* sorry. I lost a lot of my wit when you guys sucked out my brains with an Electrolux," replied Jeffrey.

The cathedral looked much as it had before. The cowardly gargoyles must have known I was coming, though, because there wasn't one in sight.

Way down at the end of the aisle, Lucifer sat behind his desk. As we approached, I could hear he was on the phone again. "How many copies? *Ten million*?!" The person on the other end explained something that made Lucifer furious. "Are you kidding me? How can they believe that stuff? It makes no sense. You have to..." He noticed me walking towards him and stopped talking in mid-sentence. He smiled Devilishly, then hung up the phone without taking his eyes off me for a second.

"Ah, Mr. Bolton. Mr. Bolton," said Lucifer, Prince of Darkness. "Weren't you supposed to bring me.... Oh, what was it now?" He comically tried to recall something. "Was it flowers? No, that's not it. A five-dollar footlong from Subway? No. Hmmmm. What could you *possibly* be missing?" he asked, his voice dripping with sarcasm.

"There was nothing I could...." I tried to explain.

"A soul, Mr. Bolton!" bellowed the Devil, his eyes burning like a furnace. "You owed me a soul. Specifically, the soul of a mass murderer who was as much of a shoe-in as Dahmer over there!" he said with a sneer toward the huge door.

"Thanks, Boss," called Jeffrey.

"I had Pizutto's pit all ready for him. I was going to chain him to the four dogs he butchered and…Oh, what's the point? Jesus has him now! A total waste of a perfectly rotten soul!" He picked up a stapler and smashed it against a marble column. He looked up toward Heaven and shouted, "I hope you're happy, Cross Boy!"

Lucifer turned his attention back to me. "Well, now I have a beautiful pit sitting all empty. Who shall I put in there, Mr. Bolton? Little Davin, perhaps?"

"No. Please, don't do that," I begged.

"Why not? That was the pawn deal, wasn't it? I permit Davin to go back to being a live little boy and you get Pizutto down here. Did that happen?"

"No," I said. "But…"

"And now that Pizutto is playing the harp and eternally out of reach, you're in default and Davin is mine. Right, Carl?"

"Well… He's just a kid, Boss," said Carl, courageously.

"'*He's just a kid*,'" Lucifer said mockingly. "You're getting soft, Boogeyman! You used to get such a kick out of scaring the pants off sweet little children. Now look at you."

Carl looked at his feet, ashamed.

"And where in Hell did you get those blasted drums?! It's worse than the banjo!" exclaimed the Devil. "Maybe I should put you in Pizutto's pit. Would you like that?"

"No," said Carl meekly.

"I'll do it," I said. "Take me. Please." I couldn't believe I was begging the Devil to sentence me to eternal torture in the land of the damned.

Lucifer thought it over. "Okay. I might very well do that. That blasted book is costing me souls by the thousands, I think I'll take you while I've got you."

Again he was complaining about a book. I had to ask, "What book are you talking about? The Bible?"

"Hah!" said the Devil. "I learned how to work around the Bible during the Dark Ages. No, this is something new. Some pastor in that country of yours wrote a book about Heaven. Apparently his son got sick and claims to have spent time playing tidily-winks with Jesus and his friends."

I thought I'd heard of it, but I was still puzzled. "Why does that bother you?"

"Because people are believing what he wrote!" he screamed.

"Is it true?"

"No. Yes. Who cares?! Millions of people have read the book and believe this kid hung out in Heaven. And they're changing their evil ways. J.C. is probably laughing at me right this moment, dammit!" He slammed his fist down on the desk, and the entire cathedral shook.

He held his head in his hands a moment, then looked up calmer. In a way, a calm Lucifer was scarier than an angry one. "Carl, please show Mr. Bolton to Raymond Pizutto's pit. And see that his dogs are brought there, too."

Carl said, "Sorry," and took hold of my arm. Lucifer turned his attention back to some papers, and Carl tried to gently guide me out. I resisted.

"Wait!" I cried. "Hold on. You're saying that kid went to Heaven?"

"I didn't say it. His father did," said Lucifer, without looking up from his paperwork.

"It's like what happened to Davin, only my boy came down here," I pointed out.

"Oooooo, what a coincidence. I have goose bumps!" said Lucifer sarcastically. "Ask me if I care?" he said, clearly tiring of the whole matter.

As hopeless as my situation was, I began to see a way out of it. I pulled away from Carl and ran up to Lucifer's desk. "I'm a writer. Let me write another book!"

Lucifer might be pure, unadulterated evil, but he's not dumb. He realized I might be on to something. "What kind of book?" he asked.

"That other guy wrote about Heaven. I'll write about Hell."

"Hmmm. What will you write?"

"I'll write what really happened to Davin and me,"

CALLING IN THE DEBT

I explained.

"Ah, nobody will believe a word of it," said Lucifer with a dismissive wave of his hand.

"Exactly! This entire story is so ludicrous no one will buy it. In fact, they'll think it's funny. They'll laugh at the entire idea and dismiss it as nonsense. And by association, people will dismiss the Heaven book, too. They'll lump them both together and they'll cancel each other out." I knew I was pushing it here, but I'd been in my share of pitch meetings and was really trying to sell him on the idea.

The Devil sat quietly and mulled it over for a while. Finally, he turned to Carl. "What do you think, Boogeyman?"

"Sounds like a plan to me. Heaven's got a book. You got a book. I like it," he said, the voice of reason.

"I like it, too!" shouted Jeffrey Dahmer's skull.

"So you'll tell the truth, which will guarantee that nobody believes it," he summarized. "Mr. Bolton, I underestimated you. You are one evil sonofabitch!"

"So..." I was afraid to ask it. "So, no pit?"

"You deliver that book to me and we can consider that debt paid in full," said Lucifer.

"Yes!" said Carl, pumping his massive fist into the air.

"Bingo!" cried Jeffrey Dahmer.

AFTERWARD

verything you've read up until this point Lucifer
read too – and approved. Oh, like anyone else, he
had a few "requests" for things to be changed. We
butted heads a bit, but eventually got through it.

Fortunately, I didn't have to make a third trip to the
Underworld. It was well after midnight when I completed
Hell Is For Real, punched Save and Print and, with a great
deal of creative pride, lumbered off to bed.

The following morning, I discovered that my manuscript
had been marked up with a red Flair. Initially I was aghast
at the desecration of my manuscript, but I soon realized that
Lucifer, besides being evil incarnate, actually had a good
grasp of grammar and story development. His corrections
and "suggestions" were really not that extensive, and it took
me only a few hours to make his adjustments. (Fair Warning:
Before you go sending angry emails to my editor, you might
want to reconsider who he really is.)

Finally, with a great sense of relief, I entered the last
fix: Lucifer wanted an exclamation point after Dahmer's
"Bingo." The moment I made that change, my office door
flew open and Davin came running in.

"Daddy, Carl came back!" he blurted. "He took the
banjo!"

That struck me as a good sign. "And did Carl give you anything important in return?" I asked hopefully.

"No," said Davin, sadly. "Just this." He handed me a red envelope.

The envelope was emblazoned with an ornate "L." Inside was a simple white card with a brief message:

Henderson, look in the trunk.

"Who's Henderson?" Davin asked.

"Who cares?!" I said, and we both tore out to my Honda.

I put the key in the lock and looked at Davin. "You ready, chief?"

Davin nodded, and I turned the key. The trunk popped open.

"Mr. Peety!!!" squealed Davin as he grabbed up the little giraffe and hugged him with all his might.

"There you go, D. I told you he'd turn up," I said. "Good as new!"

"Yeah," said Davin. "But..."

"But what son?" I asked.

He studied the giraffe carefully before saying, "Doesn't his neck seem a little longer?"

"Naw," I lied – but I doubt I'll go to Hell for it.

Well, that's the entire story. You may not believe all you've read in Hell Is For Real, but that's exactly how it happened. Perhaps you've read the other book as well. If so, you can draw your own conclusions about which is truthful and which isn't. Or perhaps you'll decide that they're both true or both totally made up. But in my experience on this globe of ours, there's usually a degree of truth and bullshit in just about everything. The challenge is figuring out how much there is of each.

Richard Bolton
May 6, 2011

About The Author
Gary Apple

Gary Apple is a New York based comedy writer who has written for many prime-time sitcoms and animated programs, including The Simpsons. He also created the popular website Stupid.com.

The author is also active in creating works for the theater. His one-act comedies have been performed throughout the United States and Canada, and he's currently a member of the BMI Musical Theater Workshop where he's creating dynamic musical comedies.

The author can be contacted through email at gary@garyapple.com.

Made in the USA
Lexington, KY
30 July 2011